BROTHERS OF WAR

a Civil War Novel by J. Marshall Martin

Boys Read Books

Boys Read Books

Published by Boys Read Books
2442 NW Market Street, Suite 214, Seattle, WA 98107

ISBN 0-9801224-0-6
Library of Congress Control Number: 2007909673
Library of Congress subject heading:
1. Civil War, 2. Andersonville, 3. Middle-grade Historical Fiction, 4.Boys Read (Organization), 5. Boys War

Printed in the United States of America
January 2008

"Future years will never know the seething hell and black infernal background, the countless minor scenes and the interiors of the secession war; and it is best they should not. The real war will never get in the books."

-- **Walt Whitman**

For my father.

CHAPTER ONE

It was neither night nor day, but a sliver of space and time in between. A dull moon sank low in a pale Georgia sky. Flames darted from torches twenty feet above a stockade wall. The smell of smoldering campfires filled the air.

I gasped a quick breath, feeling suffocated by a blanket of wooly men crammed in tight all around me. My older brother, Simon, and I waited like slaughterhouse livestock for the prison gates to open.

My mouth felt dry as dirt. I tucked my fife deep into my haversack and gripped all ten of my fingers around the back of Simon's belt.

A lonely whistle howled in the distance. I cocked my head in the direction of the railroad tracks. *How would I escape from this prison? Would I ever see Father or Kentucky again?*

Iron wheels squealed and boxcars rattled. The train I had come in on with Simon and nearly three hundred other captured Union soldiers left the depot. My heart chugged slower at the sound of the departing engine. I wished I was still on it.

The rusty hinges of the stockade gates creaked open. "Forward march, Yanks." A Rebel guard waved a burning torch. "Get moving!"

"Stay close to me, Will!" Simon's strong grip grasped my wrist like a shackle.

The men surged forward.

I clasped my fingers even tighter around my brother's belt. Sucked into a swift current of moving men, I shuffled my boots fast. Not ten paces inside the gates, a voice yelled out of the darkness, "Fresh fish! Fresh Fish! Come and get 'em, boys!"

The tightly packed men that had been crammed in all round me now split into fragments. I tried to keep pace with Simon, but tripped, stumbled, and dropped to my knees. From behind me, strong hands ripped at my haversack.

I managed to stand on my feet. I whirled around and came face-to-face with a beast of a man with wild animal eyes. His face was smoked-tar-black. His hair and beard were like tangled vines in a thicket of thorns.

"Simon!" I shouted, and dodged the man's kick.

The man's fist then thumped my chest with hard knuckles. The blow forced me backward, bouncing me off the man behind me. I flopped to the ground with a thud, and raw wind heaved from my lungs. I flipped over on my stomach, gasping for air.

"Will!" Simon's voice murmured in my throbbing eardrums. I heard nearby screams, cursing cries, and moans. Strong, fast hands scoured my pockets. Face flat in the dirt, I closed my eyes tight and lay as still as a dead man.

When all the movement around me stopped, I cracked one eye open. The man with wild animal eyes was gone. I slowly raised my head. My vision rippled as if I were looking up below the surface of shallow water. Suddenly, a huge barrel-chested man tugged on my haversack.

"No!" I crouched on my knees. "My fife!" Something smashed the side of my head. My vision squeezed closed and I stumbled into a dark tunnel.

"Will? Talk to me, Will."

It was Simon's soothing voice. The chattering of a hundred strange noises surrounded me. A foul dead-possum smell hung in the air.

I squinted open my gritty-feeling eyes. The sun scorched the inside of my skull. I strained to focus on Simon's blurry face. Thin streams of smoke swirled from campfires. My stomach growled as if a hungry dog paced inside me.

"Simon?" I mumbled through dry blood caked on my lips. "The Rebel guards robbed us!" My throat burned. My head throbbed with an aching thump.

Shaking his head, Simon helped me sit up. "Wasn't Rebs, Will. Our own kind did it; Union prisoners robbed us."

"What?" My head thumped, thumped with sharp pain.

"They were Union soldiers gone bad." Simon shook his head. "Men that have lost all their morals and code of conduct."

I craned my stiff neck, suspiciously watching the men going about their business nearby us. These prisoners passed us without a second glance. I looked around and saw a wave of men stretched as far as I could possibly see. There wasn't ten feet of open space between one man and another.

When my vision fully focused, I could see that these men looked like skeletons wearing tattered rags. Their sunken faces had barely enough skin to cover protruding, rotten teeth. Blotchy red sores and scabs covered their leathery skin. I was in a *Death Camp*.

"Both our haversacks are gone. All our food and clothes."
Simon stood taller. "I whipped one thief real good and got my
canteen and blanket back."

"My fife!" I jumped to my feet. I slapped my back searching for my haversack. "Where's my haversack?"

Simon patted my shoulder. "I said it's gone, Will."

"No! It can't be." I dropped to my hands and knees and
crawled around patting the ground with my palms trying desperately to stumble across my instrument.

The fife was my prized possession. It was no ordinary
government issued instrument. It belonged to my great-grandfather during the Revolutionary War. Great-grandfather was
only thirteen years old when he was a Fifer. Grandfather gave
the fife to Father. Father gave it to me as a present three years
ago on my eleventh birthday. I promised Father I would never
lose it!

"Ain't gonna make it," a crackly voice said.

I raised my head. A man approached. At first I thought it
was the barrel-chested man who had robbed me last night. No,
that man had been well-fed. This fellow looked like a burnt-up
cornstalk.

The cornstalk dropped his ragged trousers to his ankles
and urinated next to Simon's foot.

"Watch it!" Simon side-stepped the splash.

"By cracky, ya might make it," the cornstalk said to Simon.
"You're a cannon-stuffed with powder. Look at the size of those
shoulders. I betcha ya were born slinging an axe."

I felt like a helpless child down on my knees. I stood up
and eased closer to Simon, careful not to step on the soiled spot
on the ground draining away from the cornstalk.

"Betcha a greenback he ain't gonna make it." The man
pointed a crooked finger at me while he pulled up his trousers

with his other hand. I stepped behind Simon.

"He'll make it," Simon said.

"Well, he just might, if ya die first and I trade him to the Raiders as a slave."

Simon lunged, grabbed the man by his collar with both hands, and jerked him three inches off the ground. Six-feet tall and as lean and sturdy as a musket stock, Simon was already taller than most men. "Stay away from my brother!"

The cornstalk's eyes bugged out like a grasshopper's.

"No, Simon." I grabbed Simon's elbows and pulled hard. "Let him go."

Released from Simon's grip, the man stepped back and rubbed his neck. Simon's fingers left white marks on the man's dirty skin. "You'll make it, sure enough," the man said, and stuck out his hand. "I'm Badger, Wisconsin Cavalry."

Neither Simon nor I offered our hands.

I straightened my shoulders, lifted my chin, and looked him in the eye. "We're the Taylors, Ninth Kentucky Volunteer Infantry."

"Welcome to Andersonville Prison." Badger smiled a tobacco-rotten grin. "Whatcha got the Raiders ain't took?"

"Raiders?" Simon rubbed the back of his head.

"Thieves that whipped ya last night," Badger said. "We call 'em Raiders."

Simon picked up his blue woolen blanket and lifted his wooden canteen.

"Trade ya a knife for that blanket." Badger leaned closer.

"Not for trade." Simon tucked the blanket tight under his arm.

"Blade comes mighty handy in here. Think it over, ya ain't goin' nowhere."

"We'll escape!" I said.

"Nobody escapes. Most men die in a week. If ya want to live, ya boys better listen to me." Badger scratched his chin as if thinking hard. "Reckon ya could join the Tribe. We're a pack of men who live with a big Indian. We call him Chief. We call ourselves the Tribe. We could use a couple of new fellas."

I looked at Simon. He shrugged.

"Our camp's over yonder, down Main Street." Badger pointed to a road that cut through the center of the stockade. "Look for the big Indian. Ya can't miss 'em."

He saluted us with a wide grin, abruptly did an about-face and lumbered away with widespread legs like he had a large chunk of saddle permanently wedged between his thighs.

"Walks like cavalry," I said.

"Smells like cavalry, too." Simon clipped his nose with two fingers. "I've smelled pack-mules better than him."

I snorted, trying to blow clots of crusty blood from my nose holes. I rubbed the knot on the side of my head where the boot had landed. My ribs ached when I breathed too deep. I had to take short breaths. I felt pinned down and trapped in an airless boxcar. I wanted to search for my fife right away, but I was too tired, sore, and hungry to try.

CHAPTER TWO

"There's got to be a crack or hole in the wall somewhere to escape," Simon said. He stood on his tiptoes trying to see above the heads of other prisoners.

I twisted my stiff neck back and forth as if I had been bucked and fell from a horse. I didn't see any cracks or holes. All I saw were men. The men never stopped moving. They were like over-crowded chickens pecking around for tiny seeds.

"Come on, Will," Simon said. "Let's scout this place out."

Simon never waited for me. When he set his mind to something, he would just take off and do it! That's how I got into this mess in the first place. After Father joined the Union army, Simon followed him the same day he turned seventeen. I wasn't going to be left behind in Kentucky. The only way the army would take me was as a *Fifer* in the band.

I didn't let Simon get more than three feet ahead of me as we worked our way through a crowd of men. We stopped on the highest ground we could find. It was only a small knoll, but we could now see the lay of the stockade. The land stretched between two low-rising hills.

A narrow creek bordered by several yards of swampy mud cut through the center of the prison grounds. Stumps littered the bare soil. The only thing that was growing was men. They were popping up as if they were insects crawling out from nest-holes in the earth.

The prison walls were made from tall and scraggly pine logs wedged upright, side-by-side. Streams of black campfire smoke dotted acre upon acre of barren ground. The cooking smell of the fires made my stomach rumble with hunger. "The camp looks like one big Indian village," I said.

"There must be over ten thousand men in here," Simon said as he scouted the land with his hand shielding his brow. "More men than I ever saw on a battlefield. They're crawling around the camp like hungry flies on fresh buffalo kill."

I nodded. Simon's words sounded muffled and distant as if they drifted from the center of thick cannon smoke. All I could think about was my stolen fife. On my tiptoes, I scanned the camp. I listened for music and looked for a glimmer of shiny metal.

"Let's get moving." Simon pulled on my sleeve.

I felt the tug, but barely heard him.

"Hey, Lunkhead! Let's get. I want to find a way out of here before nightfall."

"What? Find what?" I asked.

Simon shook my shoulders and squared me up eye-to-eye. "Snap out of it, Will. You look like you've gone stone cold on me. I need you to be battlefield-ready!"

"I'm ready, but I need to find my fife."

"Forget it, Lunkhead. That fife won't help us escape. If we stumble across it, so be it. But we can't waste time on it."

I twisted away from Simon and shouted, "I see something

shiny." I charged down the hill, tripped over my own feet, rolled headfirst into a summersault, bounced back up, and regained my balance.

An old man squatted, plunging something into the dirt. "That's my fife!" I shoved him with my palms, knocking the old man backward.

Simon reached my side and grabbed my arm. "It's a spoon. Just a dirty spoon, Will."

I lowered my chin and stared at a long, silver serving spoon caked with dirt.

"Spoon don't mean nothin' to me," the old man pleaded. He rocked back and forth, pulling his skinny legs to his chest. "Don't beat me! Spoon don't mean nothin' to me. You can have it. I'll steal another from the Bake House. Good for diggin' grub worms." The man popped a small yellow worm he held between two fingers into his mouth. "Want a worm? I'll dig ya one."

With my head still lowered, I walked away in silence. I wasn't hungry anymore. When I could finally talk again, I said, "That Badger fellow was right, Simon. We're not going to escape this place, and I'm not going to survive in here."

"I won't have that kind of talk, Will Taylor." Simon straightened his spine and raised his chin high. "We'll make it. We survived the battlefields of Stone's River and Chickamauga. We won't breathe our last breath in this rotten place. We'll see Father in Kentucky again. You can mark my word on that."

I nodded, but I knew good and well that I might never see Father or Kentucky again.

We kept moving and made our way to Main Street. Hundreds of men packed a street not much wider than a wagon. I took quick glances at the other prisoners. I still couldn't believe these were living souls. I had seen lots of dead men on the battlefields in the last three years since I had left Kentucky. I got used to seeing them; after awhile they were all alike. They were dead and I wasn't.

But, here in the stockade, the dead and the living seemed strangely the same.

A wagon pulled by two mules rolled down the center of Main. Simon and I stepped aside. Wobbly wheels squeaked. The wagon headed south, was loaded with corpses. It was hard to imagine these men had been living only hours ago. Most of the bodies were half-skeleton, half-flesh, with elbows, knees, feet, and hands all twisted and mangled like scrap fence wire.

We lowered our heads in respect for the dead. When the wagon had passed, Simon said, "There's the tall Indian about a hundred yards on the left."

"Where?" I stood on my tiptoes. "I don't see him."

"You're too short." Simon pointed. "There's Badger, too. Let's check it out."

I inched behind Simon as we approached the Tribe's encampment.

Badger poked his long neck up high as a prairie dog. "By cracky, if it ain't the Kentucky boys."

The big Indian raised his head from where he was scrubbing clothes in a bucket of sandy colored water. His wide eyes were like dull coins. He nodded and went back to work.

"Hey Hoosier, Buckeye, come on out of your hole," Badger called in the direction of one of the makeshift tents.

Two men crawled out. One of them wasn't much older than Simon. He only had one arm. The other man looked like a nervous coon treed by a pack of hounds. His eyes darted back and forth, never landing on any one thing.

These men were different from the other prisoners. Their clothes were worn with age, but clean. They were skinny, but still had some meat on their bones. Most of all, their eyes held a glimmer of hope.

"These boys are fresh fish, by golly," Badger said. "Kentuckians."

The young man with one arm extended his hand to Simon. "I'm Buckeye, Fifty-ninth Ohio."

"Simon Taylor." Simon shook the boy's hand. "This is my brother, Will."

I shook hands with Buckeye, trying not to look at his stumped arm. I liked Buckeye's firm grip. It was strong and confident.

The nervous man just stood there smiling as if he had won a prize. His eyes never came to rest on anyone or anything. He seemed too happy for this place.

"Come on over, Hoosier," Badger said. "Two new Kentucky boys for ya to meet. They won't bite ya."

Hoosier raised his hand and waved to me. "Apple pie, Ma makes the best apple pie. Stack your muskets. Cows! Cows out of the field! Gotta get those cows!" Hoosier turned, ducked down, and crawled back inside his tent.

Badger chuckled. "Ain't he a work. Indiana farmer. Volunteered for artillery. Nineteenth Indiana Battery. Been like that ever since Chief found 'em. Think a shell rattled his bucket."

I glanced over at Chief, who relentlessly scrubbed a shirt so thin it appeared his thick fingers would poke right through it.

"You can lay your blanket right next to my shebang," Buckeye said.

Simon's knuckles whitened as he tightened his grip on his blanket. "What's a shebang?"

"Tents." Buckeye pointed to their makeshift shelters. "Made from whatever you can scrounge up within the stockade walls."

"Most men don't live long enough to need a shebang," Badger said. "We lost two last week. One got paroled. The other exchanged."

"Exchanged!" I stepped closer. "How do you get exchanged? We need to get out of here."

Badger burst out laughing and slapped Buckeye on the back. "Good gosh oh mighty, the boys are fresh. Take good care of these boys, I'm off to trade." He disappeared into a mass of men chattering and bickering on Main Street.

"Exchanged is what we say when you just up and die," Buckeye explained. "Most men die of disease and starvation. Paroled is what happens when a guard shoots you. See those boys up in that pigeon-roost?"

I looked up at two Rebel guards high in a sentry box on the parapet. The guards' hairless faces appeared even younger than mine. "Stay away from the Deadline and you won't get paroled," Buckeye said.

"Deadline?" I questioned.

"It's that railing strung out there, 'bout twenty feet out from the wall." Buckeye pointed with his one hand.

I turned to see a weathered rope that was tied to a fence post marking the boundary of the Deadline. The Tribes' tents were only a few yards away from the line.

"Captain Wirz has any man shot who crosses that rope," Buckeye said. "He's the commander of the prison. Scared we might storm the wall with a ladder or something." He chuckled. "Nothing but bones in here to make a ladder with."

"We can dig out!" I said. "I saw a man with a spoon digging. We have to escape!"

CHAPTER THREE

"There's no escaping," Buckeye said. "You just survive."

"We have to escape." I walked in a circle as if I were a mule tied to a post. "How do you escape?"

Buckeye grasped my arm. I tried to pull away, but his grip was too tight. "To escape, you get food first. You got to stay healthy, clean, and strong. That's how you escape death." Buckeye lifted his stump arm. "This is what I got from trying to escape."

Pink scar tissue circled his elbow. "I got gangrene after being locked in the Stocks. You don't want your neck locked in the Stocks in this heat, do you?"

Buckeye released his grip. I shook my head and dabbed my fingers across my neck. My eyes darted back and forth, watching the prisoners trading on Main Street.

"Onions, turnips, potatoes," Buckeye rattled off. "If there's no food, take anything you can get to trade for food: shirts, belts, socks, bootlaces." He paused like he was making sure his words were sinking in.

"Food first." I eagerly nodded.

"Guards trade, too. Johnny Rebs like our Union buttons. 'Buttons with hens,' they call them. Just dumb old country boys. Don't even know it's an American Eagle on our buttons. Remember the Deadline. Make them come to you."

"Eagles." I fiddled with the buttons on my jacket. I was proud to have Eagles.

Buckeye puffed his chest out and said, "If you don't remember anything else, remember this: don't drink the water at the Stinks."

Simon stepped closer. "What are the Stinks?"

Buckeye pointed at the swampy creek where we had met Badger earlier. "New men die first because they break down and drink the nasty water. Creek's a latrine. It goes through the guards' camp before it ever gets to us. No matter how hot it gets, don't drink it! We get some good spring water from the guards. But when it rains, we capture all the water we can."

I reached over, picked up Simon's canteen, and swished it around. I was relieved Simon still had some water left.

"All us Indians got a job to do in the Tribe. Chief's no businessman. He only does the washing. Men trade with Chief for doing their laundry. Staying clean is important, too. Clean men don't get the sores like the dirty men do. That's why Chief's laundry business is booming.

Badger's one of the best peddler's in the stockade. He's got a silver tongue. Full of bull — talk the socks right out of your boots before you even know it. I keep the books. Write things down for Chief. Keep my eyes on supplies — Quartermaster, you might say. Hoosier makes us laugh."

I craned my neck to see Hoosier's shebang. I hadn't heard a word from him since he went after his cows.

"Don't get me wrong. We don't laugh at Hoosier," Buckeye

said. "Don't make fun of him, either. We laugh all together. Chief will kick the tar out of you for poking at Hoosier."

I glanced over at Chief. Chief never raised his head from the endless scrubbing. His massive forearms were like thick axe handles.

"Here comes Tall Paul now with a stump," Buckeye said.

I eased closer to Simon. Tall Paul was even taller than Chief. He carried a stump under one arm.

"Got two new Indians," Buckeye said to Tall Paul.

Tall Paul drooped over and stuck out his hand. It looked like an enormous bear paw, stained orange from digging in the dirt. A wide grin spread across his lips. I instantly liked him, and extended my hand.

"I'm Will. Will Taylor." Tall Paul's gentle grip surprised me.

"Paul. Paul Mattox, Iowa Infantry." His voice was melodic as a note from my fife.

Simon rose up on his tiptoes as if he was trying to be as tall as Tall Paul. "I'm Simon!" His eyes were wild with excitement.

I could tell that Simon was ready to jump into the thick of things. It wasn't like him to sit and wait for something to come to him.

"Roots make for good soup," Buckeye said.

"Root soup tonight," said Tall Paul.

I cocked my head to the right. "Hear that?"

"Hear what?" asked Simon.

"I heard a fife!" I twisted around and stood high on my tiptoes.

"You can't hear a cannon blast with all the racket in this place," Simon said.

"I know my own fife when I hear it!" I pushed past Simon

and scurried out into the center of Main Street. "My fife!"

"Where?" Simon scanned the street.

"Those three men coming our way. The red-faced man in the middle's got it!"

"Sure?" Simon stepped closer to me.

"I've got to get it back, Simon! You know that. I have to talk with those men."

Buckeye grabbed me with death-grip fingers. "Men like that don't reason. Let it go."

"I can't." I spoke directly to Simon. "You know I can't. That fife belongs to our family. I promised Father I would never lose it!"

The three men were stout Raiders. They laughed, cursed, bumped, and pushed other prisoners out of their way. The red-faced man in the middle twirled my fife between his hands.

A short, bald man flanked the middle man's right and on the left side was a man I recognized. It was the man with wild-animal eyes!

Simon took a quick swig from his canteen. His eyes narrowed and his lips sucked back to his teeth. I knew the expression well. I called it Simon's trigger-face.

I sucked in a deep breath and tried to swallow, but the walls of my throat felt as if they were coated with dry gunpowder.

When the Raiders were only a few paces away, Simon stepped in front of them. "That's a nice fife you got there," Simon said to the red-faced man.

The men paused, looked at each other with scrunched up faces. My heart rattled like a battle drum. I stood two feet behind Simon. I glanced to my side. Buckeye was gone.

A wobbly feeling churned my stomach like soured buttermilk. The only member of the Tribe I could see was Chief. With his head down, Chief kept on scrubbing.

The red-faced Raider with the fife then spit a large splat of tobacco out. "Reckon it's a nice fife. Traded for it last night."

"And it was a darn good trade," the bald Raider said. "All he gave for it was a cup of moldy beans."

I clenched my jaws tight to keep my mouth shut and lowered my head to avoid looking directly into the wild-animal eyes.

"Does it work?" Simon asked.

"Oh yeah. It's a dandy," the red-faced Raider said.

"I'll trade you this canteen for it." Simon extended his wooden canteen like a hand shake.

All three men burst out laughing. Simon's eyes narrowed. I stepped another foot closer.

The red-faced Raider tapped the fife in his palm like a stick. "You want a trade," he said, "but you ain't got nothin' I want."

His sidekicks laughed.

"It's my fife!" I anchored myself beside Simon. "You stole it from me last night. I want it back!"

"Shut up, Lunkhead." Simon pushed the canteen into my hand. "Take this and get over to the Chief."

My feet were stuck in a rut, my hand trembled, and I dropped the canteen.

"I do believe that young boy's calling you a thief," Wild-animal eyes said. "He's insulted your honor, Captain."

The red-faced Raider with the fife stood taller. He saluted the other two men with the fife. "Do pardon me gentlemen, but a Captain's honor must be defended." He turned to me. "I demand an apology, boy."

I balled my fist. Out of the corner of my eye, I could see that Simon's fists were cocked tight to his chest.

"You apologize now or I'm going to bend you over my knee and tan your hide," Red-faced said. "What kind of manners did your father teach you, boy?"

"Back off!" Simon stepped forward with his fists clenched in front of his chest.

Red-faced stepped forward, too.

Simon stood his ground. I wanted to run, but dared not leave my brother.

The man tapped Simon on his fist with the tip of my fife. "Get out of my way, before I knock you out of my way!"

"Let's go, Simon." I pulled on his sleeve. "I don't want that old fife anymore."

Simon nudged me further away. "You get gone, Will Taylor."

"Let's see what these boys are made of," Red-face said, and spit tobacco on Simon's boot. Simon lurched forward, shoved the man in the chest, and snatched the fife faster than a rattlesnake.

Red-face stumbled backward and his friends caught him before he hit the ground.

"Run, Will!" Simon yelled.

I twisted around, ran a few steps, and stopped when I heard Simon cry out in pain. I looked behind me.

Simon was pinned on the ground with Red-face on top of him.

The fife was on the ground, too.

All sounds stopped in my head. I pivoted left and pivoted right. I eyed my fife barely four feet from me. It was still too close to the Raiders to grab it.

Simon squirmed free from Red-face's grip and made it back to his feet. He jumped up and down with raised fists in the air like a madman. "Come on! I'll whip all of you!"

All three of the Raiders closed in on Simon like a tightening lasso.

Simon's teeth sucked tight to his lips. I had seen him whip

two boys at the same time, but these were full-grown men.

Wild-animal eyes charged and hit Simon in the chest with a full-shoulder punch. Simon collapsed. The bald man pounced on Simon's back. Red-face locked his arm around Simon's neck. Simon chomped down on Red-face's hand with his teeth and Red-face let out a howl of pain.

"Hooray!" I jumped with raised fist in the air.

The bald man managed to wrap his arms around Simon's kicking legs. Wild-animal eyes kicked Simon right in the nose. Simon's head snapped back.

"Chief!" I waved. "Help us, Chief!"

Chief didn't even raise his head.

I ran closer to Chief. "Let's whip these Raiders!"

Chief looked up. His black eyes looked cold as a kettle. He turned his back on me.

"No Chief! We need your help!"

When Chief didn't respond, I ran down the edge of Main searching the painful faces of other men for mercy. "Somebody help us! Please somebody help!"

No one moved.

Out of the corner of my eye, I spotted my fife again. I ran to it, and scooped it up. I took two long strides and jumped onto the back of Wild-animal eyes. He had Simon's shoulder pinned to the ground with his knees. His hands were grasped around Simon's neck. With my one free hand, I tugged hard on the man's long hair. I held my fife firmly with my other hand.

Wild-animal eyes grunted, wheeled around in a circle and slung me to the ground. I rolled over on my back. He dropped down and straddled my waist with his legs, grasped my neck with both hands, and tightly squeezed.

I gasped for air. The rough-feeling hands collapsed around my throat. I gagged and felt like I was being held under water;

I tried to yell, but nothing left my mouth. My sight faded to a grayish-white.

At that moment, my eyes expanded larger and a surge of energy swelled inside me when I spotted a familiar looking medallion tied around the man's neck. The medallion dangled before my blurry vision. *Could it be Father's?*

I crammed the tip of my fife under the man's jaw and twisted my neck free. I sucked in a wave of quick breaths.

"Simon!" My weak arms trembled.

"Will!" Simon's voice was close.

Loud footsteps thumped and a sudden force hit the man on top of me in his back and thrust him forward. The man screamed as if he had been pierced by a bayonet.

Something sticky oozed down my fife onto my hand and wrist. I rolled away from the man with my right hand securely gripping the fife. The instrument was streaked with a white and red liquid. *Was it blood?*

Suddenly, the bald Raider and Red-face backed away.

Chief and Tall Paul stood like giant trees in the street. Both held clubs. Buckeye was behind them with a Bowie knife raised in the air with his one arm.

I tucked my knees tight to my chest and clutched my fife with both hands. I spotted Simon.

Simon knelt on his knees. His head was tilted back and blood trickled from his nose.

"We won!" I triumphantly raised my fife above my head, but my smug satisfaction faded to pity at the sound of a man moaning.

Wild-animal eyes squirmed on the dirt. "My eye! My eye!"

My neck was throbbing raw. I gently stroked the skin under my chin. I had to get a closer look at the medal still around the man's neck. *Could it be Father's?*

I crawled on my hands and knees, clutching my fife in my right fist. The man's screaming was like a hot poker sizzling my nerves. I forced myself to look more closely.

The man had both palms cupped over his injured eye. White and red ooze streaked the man's hands. I knew the tip of my fife had gouged his eye.

I inched closer for a better look. I couldn't believe it! It was a bronze medal about the size of a silver dollar, just like Father's. I squinted hard and could clearly see a distinct hairline crack at the top of the medal.

"Yes!" I shouted. My lungs breathed faster with excitement. "It's Father's!" No doubt about it; I could see the smooth, worn surface of the two patriots shaking hands in the center of the medal.

I reached for the medallion, but a strong hand grabbed my collar and pulled me back.

"Don't touch him!" It was Red-face.

I tried to speak, but my windpipe felt closed. I looked over to Simon and saw that Tall Paul and Chief were helping him to his feet.

"Thou shalt reap what thou hast sown," the bald Raider said.

"I didn't do it on purpose," I pleaded. "It just happened."

The bald man and Red-face both turned to face Simon.

"He didn't do it, either!" I said.

"It was your stick, boy," Red-face said to me. "Gonna cut your eye out, fry it like a fat oyster."

"It wasn't a stick." I stood up. "It was my fife." I held my fife out. "It was an accident. I just wanted my fife back."

Red-face and the bald man helped their injured friend to his feet and led him away.

"It was an accident!" I raised my fife in the air. "It was a fife, not a stick, see?"

Red-face stopped and turned back around to face me. "Accident or not, we're going to get you, boy. It's an eye for an eye in Andersonville!"

CHAPTER FOUR

Back with the safety of the Tribe, I sat beside Simon on the blue blanket, dabbing his cuts clean with a handkerchief. My fife was tucked firmly under my right leg.

"Ouch." Simon raised his head. "Don't press so hard."

"Sorry." I scooted closer and dabbed more gently. "Simon, you didn't put that man's eye out. I didn't do it either. Maybe we should ask Badger to help us talk some sense into those men. He's a slick talker."

"He can't help us, Will. Just drop it! You got your fife back."

I turned my head away and stared out into a hazy, gray sky. I couldn't help but to think of Father. If his medal was here, he might be here, too. I wanted to tell Simon about seeing Father's medal, but knew that it was too soon. Simon needed to heal first before getting involved in another fight. If he knew that man had Father's medal, he would be after him without a thought. I glanced over to Chief.

Chief crouched over his wash pan only a few feet away,

vigorously scrubbing laundry. Buckeye scribbled notes in his ledger. Hoosier sat cross-legged next to Buckeye, folding laundry and mumbling to himself. Tall Paul knocked clumps of dirt from his stump with thick fingers.

"Here comes Badger." Simon sat higher. "Don't trust him."

"I don't." I pushed my fife even further under my leg.

"Thundering trumpets." Badger stepped onto the edge of Simon's blanket with muddy boots.

Simon glared his trigger-face. "Your boots are muddy, get off my blanket."

Badger sidestepped off the blanket with wide bowlegs and saluted Simon. "Yes sir, Sergeant Simon." Badger opened his arms out like he was delivering a sermon to the Tribe. "These here Kentucky boys done made a name for themselves."

Chief, Buckeye, and Hoosier all perked up and listened to Badger speak. "Not in camp half a day and they're a legend bigger than fierce John Brown himself."

Badger reached in his pockets and pulled out two potatoes and three turnips. He tossed the vegetables into the air and juggled them singing, "Taters and turnips, taters and turnips, all we got's taters and turnips. Put 'em in your root soup and cook 'em up good." He tossed them one by one into an iron kettle that Tall Paul was using over a campfire to boil his tree stump.

Tall Paul leaned away from the splashing vegetables.

"Yes-sir-ree, Willy boy." Badger skipped over and put his arm around me. "The camp has already nicknamed that Raider ya butchered, Fog Eye."

"I didn't butcher anyone." I twisted away and crossed my arms tightly over my chest.

Badger leaned closer to me and spoke in a trembling hush: "I seen it. Nothin' but a foggy mist floatin' around his eyeball.

He's hot on ya, Willy boy. Can't quit talkin' about ya."

I turned away from his sour-smelling breath. "It was an accident," I said loudly, not even looking at Badger.

"It's whatever ya say it is, partner." Badger patted my shoulder. "Ya can call it whatever ya want. And don't ya worry none, Badger will take good care of ya."

"Line 'em up," a voice ordered deep from the center of a crowd of men.

I turned to see a group of fast-marching Rebel sentries. "Line 'em up! Line 'em up, men," the guards called. "You know the routine."

Buckeye and Tall Paul helped Simon to his feet. We lined up on Main Street with all the other prisoners.

"Time for the daily headcount," Buckeye said.

"Here comes Lincoln." Hoosier stood tall and saluted.

"What in tarnation is he talking about now?" I asked Buckeye.

"He thinks Captain Wirz is President Lincoln," Buckeye said. I looked down the street and saw Captain Wirz riding a white horse. He jostled around on his saddle holding onto the reins with his left hand. His right arm was in a black sling. His starched uniform creased like crisp paper.

"Union forces at the battle of Seven Pines shattered his elbow," Buckeye said. "Blames all us Yankees for it. He's as mean as a stirred hornet."

"Guards, watch these Yankees!" Wirz called out. "Blind fools. These men are playing tricks!" He wheeled his horse around.

I was surprised to see Tall Paul and Badger answer their names during the roll call, get their daily rations, then duck behind the other men. They scurried down to the far end of the line and answered the roll again for two men that were either dead or too sick to make it out for their rations.

"No more rations today! I'll teach you prisoners to play tricks." Wirz guided his horse in a revolving circle.

A man who had not yet received his rations screamed out, "You flying chicken turd. Try coming in here without your guards. We'll skin and eat you like the stinking rat you are."

Wirz pulled his reins to the left. "You won't play games with me again!"

"Go milk your goat with your nose," a prisoner yelled far down the line.

"You insolent animal! You'll all die here." Wirz galloped away.

"What did Lincoln say?" Hoosier asked.

"You better listen to the Captain boys," a guard said. "Bringing in some dignitaries and women tomorrow from Macon. No telling what he'll do to you, if you don't straighten up."

The prisoners dispersed from the roll call. Back at our shebangs, we all divvied up what little rations we had collected between us. Luckily, Tall Paul and Badger got double rations with their trick, and every member of the Tribe had at least a little something to eat.

I spent the rest of my first day at Andersonville on the blue woolen blanket. I didn't dare leave the safety of the Tribe. I polished my fife with my shirttail until it shined. Simon lay with his eyes closed. I wanted desperately to tell him about Father's medal.

Chief's washing operation boomed with business. Men came with filthy laundry, men left with semi-clean laundry. Chief scrubbed. That's all he did. Scrub. Scrub. Scrub. Never talked. Never smiled. Rarely looked up.

Buckeye kept track of every article that came in, every article that went out. Hoosier spent the rest of the day in his shebang. He was alone, but I could hear him incessantly talking.

Tall Paul left for short periods and always came back covered in red dirt like he had been digging for more roots.

That evening, when Tall Paul's soup was ready to serve, Buckeye gave Simon and me two homemade wooden spoons. They were covered with grit. I scrubbed the spoons in the cleanest of the dirty laundry water and dried them with my shirttail. I wondered if I should have kept the silver kitchen spoon the worm-eating man had offered me.

Simon's wooden canteen was empty. Buckeye took his Bowie knife and split the canteen down the middle, making each of us a dish for our root soup. When the wood snapped in half, I felt splinters run up my spine. I ran my fingers over the rough edge of the bowl. The two halves made me feel separated from Simon. I scooted closer to my big brother.

The root soup wasn't too bad. It turned out Tall Paul was a fine cook. The best part about the soup was the boiled potatoes and turnips. Buckeye saw that everybody in the Tribe got equal portions. He dished out the soup from a small tin cup that had a pinhole size leak in it. He held half a wooden canteen under the leak, so that he was sure not lose a drop of soup.

Not a thimble of root soup was left when we were done eating. We used crusty, hardtack biscuits to sop up every bit. I inched closer to the warm flames of the campfire. My belly felt full. My stomach had shrunk so it didn't take much food to fill me these days. I hadn't had much to eat since Simon and I had been captured.

Later that evening, Badger got a brown, quart-sized bottle from inside his shebang and popped it open by the fire. He turned the bottle up and took a gurgling guzzle. "Holy water." He wiped his mouth on his sleeve. "Best Pine-Top whisky in the stockade. Couple of boys from Boston boiled it up. One's a mason, the other is a blacksmith. Rigged a whole blasted steel down yonder by the Dead House. Perfect hiding place. No man alive dare go by there."

Maybe Father's hiding in the Dead House? I leaned close to Simon, but held my tongue.

"Want a swig, Simon?" Badger said.

"No thanks." Simon looked away.

"Ahh, come on, have a drink with the Badge." He shoved the bottle of Pine-Top over to Simon.

Simon turned to Buckeye with raised eyebrows.

"It won't hurt you," Buckeye said.

"It won't help you, either," Tall Paul said. "But I drink it anyway. Give me a swig."

Badger passed the bottle.

Tall Paul held the bottle up to the firelight. I could see swirling particles floating inside.

"Hellfire, take a soldier's pull. You'll like it." Badger grinned.

Chief's big arms were crossed over his chest. He kept an eye on Hoosier, who was crawling around on his hands and knees like he was looking for something.

"Take a soldier's drink. Ya deserve it," Badger said. "Ya cooked us a fine stump."

Tall Paul eased the bottle up to his lips and took a small sip. "That ain't no count," Badger said. "Take a pull. Take a soldier's pull!"

Tall Paul tilted the bottle down his throat, coughed, and spewed a mist of whisky right in Badger's face. Everyone burst out laughing.

Chief smiled. "No good."

"Tastes like turpentine." Tall Paul spat and rubbed his mouth on his shirtsleeve.

"It mostly is." Badger shuffled his feet and danced around

the fire laughing, slapping his knees.

"Watch out!" Hoosier pushed Badger. "You almost stepped on Lola."

Badger stood still with a sober face. "Where is she?"

"Right by your left boot," Hoosier said. "Watch where you step. They're real little."

"Golly, she is, ain't she." Badger squatted, his face was calm and compassionate. "Is that Leroy between her?"

"That's him." Hoosier bent over and cupped a handful of dirt by Badger's feet.

No one said a word. The fire crackled.

Chief's long jaw rested on his chest.

Buckeye leaned over to me. "Hoosier's got two pet Graybacks, Lola and Leroy."

"Thought Graybacks were Rebels," I said.

"Lice," Buckeye answered. "Chief loves them. It's his favorite thing Hoosier does."

"Mind if I hold 'em?" Badger asked.

Hoosier dumped dirt into Badger's open palm. I stood and strained to see Leroy and Lola.

"Hello darlin', Lola," Badger said in a soft voice. "How ya doin' old boy, Leroy? Takin' good care of the little lady?"

"How about we play a game of Even-odd tonight, Badger?" Tall Paul said.

"What ya got worth taking?" Badger asked and handed Hoosier the dirt that held Leroy and Lola.

Tall Paul pulled a knife out from under his shirt. "Got an Arkansas toothpick." The knife had a long, skinny blade like a pick.

"I've got a looking glass to trade," Badger said.

"Does it work?" Tall Paul asked.

"Ya betcha," Badger said. "I can see clear to the railroad

tracks with it."

"Best of three," Tall Paul said.

"Best of three, on three," Badger said.

Tall Paul nodded and counted, "One, two, three, even."

Both men reached up under their shirts, pinched around in several spots, pulled their hands out, and held their palms open.

Tall Paul groaned after counting his lice. "Got three, odd."

"Two!" Badger clapped his hands. "Even's winner."

Simon laughed, bobbing his head. I lifted my shirt up and searched for critters. "I don't have any lice. How can I play Even-odd?"

"Don't worry." Buckeye chuckled. "You've only been here a day. You'll have critters camping all over you soon."

Simon stood. "We won't be here long enough for that."

"Food first," Buckeye said.

"Food first," Simon said, nodding.

Badger and Tall Paul played two more rounds of Even-odd. Badger swept Tall Paul and won the knife.

"Play us something on your fife, Will," Buckeye said.

My fife rested on my lap. I reached down and tucked my shirt over it. "I'm not up for playing."

Chief lifted his chin and stared right at me with his black eyes.

I shifted my eyes away from Chief.

"Ain't that something," Badger said. "Willy boy risks his life for an old fife, and he can't even play a lick on it."

"I can play it just fine," I snapped.

Simon placed a hand on my shoulder and gave a comforting squeeze. "Go ahead, play."

I nodded, licked my lips, and two soft warm-up notes

blew from my fife. I wet my lips a little more and said, "Any requests?"

"How about *Rally Around The Flag, Boys*?" Tall Paul said.

"That's an easy song to play," I said, and took a deep breath. I played.

All eyes were on me. Badger swigged from his bottle.

"Now that was dandy," Buckeye said. "Good to have some real music back in the Tribe. Last drummer we had couldn't play nothing but battle beats."

I felt proud. Next I played *Lorena*.

"That song sure enough was purty, but the Badge is turning it in boys." He pointed the Arkansas toothpick at Simon. "Don't forget, a blade comes in mighty handy in here." He handed the knife handle first to Simon.

Simon took it and plunged the blade in the ground between his feet.

Badger put one hand on my shoulder. "Sleep with one eye open, Willy boy. Fog Eye's liable to be on the prowl tonight. Death will follow ya now like your own shadow. Ya ain't escaping it. It'll follow ya right into your dreams."

I cringed and felt my knuckles tighten around my fife.

Badger slinked away and ducked inside his shebang with his bottle.

"More," Chief said.

Startled, I glanced up. Chief stared at the campfire. I tried to track his dark eyes, but found no signs to follow.

"Play more." Simon nudged me. "You heard Chief."

I wonder what Chief would like to hear? After much thought, I chose, *Home, Sweet Home*. I played with my eyes closed.

When I finished playing the song, I opened my eyes. Everyone was asleep except Simon and Hoosier. Simon stared into the sky. Hoosier sat outside his shebang whispering to Leroy and Lola in his shirt pocket.

It was a murky night. The stars and moon were smothered behind strangling clouds. I closed my eyes, cocked my head, and tried to make out the tune of distant banjo music. The sounds of drifting voices, coughing, moaning, and crying cluttered the air. Within seconds of closing my eyes, a haunting image of Fog Eye crept into my mind. My eyes instantly popped open, and I alertly scanned the dark fringes of camp. Every pop of pine-knot in nearby campfires forced me to check over my shoulder.

CHAPTER FIVE

Later that night, I curled close to Simon on the bare ground with only the blue blanket covering my legs. I lay flat on my back with my eyes wide open. I hid my fife under the bend of my knees. I twisted and rolled back and forth trying to fall asleep, but couldn't. *Was Father in the prison somewhere?*

When I finally fell asleep, inside my dreamy mind, gray smoke twisted from a cannon barrel. Thunder rumbled. Cold rain splattered, sending a chill deep into my bones.

"*Simon...*" I was trapped underneath the surface of my dream. I tried to break loose, but couldn't wake up. "*Simon? Got to find Simon!*"

I searched a ravaged Chickamauga battlefield for my brother. It was the same dream I had had many nights since the horrific battle. Stepping over the head of an artillery horse, I paused at Chickamauga Creek. The current swirled with spilled blood. I stared at the water. A decapitated head of a man floated by like a child's rolling ball. I twisted away, but had to look back. The face was familiar, but I couldn't make it out. I hurried down the bank following the head. It spun around and around. I grabbed a long stick from the ground, reached out and poked the head, trying to roll the face closer to the bank.

"*Double-quick!*" Colonel Cram's voice ordered commands deep within the blinding smoke. Startled, I jumped and dropped my stick in the creek.

"*Double-quick, left in front!*" The bugles cried sharp and insistent. "*Fix bayonets!*"

Canisters hurled overhead, shredding leaves from the trees. Exploding missiles splattered dirt. I fell to the ground behind a dead horse and covered my head.

A half-wolf, half-Indian sound screeched. It was the Rebel Yell. "*Retreat! Retreat!*"

I stood and stared in the creek. The floating head was gone. "*Simon!*" I would not leave Simon on the battlefield. I stumbled forward, stepped in a hole, and sunk. I kicked, grabbed, flailed, and sank deeper. I stretched my arms far from my sides and tried to stop the sliding. The more I struggled, the faster I sank. I reached for a tree root dangling at the edge of the hole. Right when I grabbed the root, a rat with pointy teeth scurried up and bit my knuckles.

My arms thrust into the air, and I yelled, "*Simon!*"

Simon grabbed my hands and pulled up. I looked down into the hole. The floating head was back! Father's face rolled over and over with wide dead eyes. "*Father!*"

Now awake, I kicked and grabbed at something being pulled off of me. "No!"

I could see the shadowy figure of Simon. "That's my blanket!" Simon chased two men down Main Street. I shivered from the chill of night. Simon returned clutching his blue woolen blanket. "They slid the blanket right out from under our noses," Simon said.

The soles of my socks were cold touching the ground. "They stole my boots, too," I said.

In the morning Badger led a regiment of men to the Tribe. "Here they is, boys." A sly grin slid across Badger's face like greasy gravy. "Fresh Fish from the ninth Kentucky Vols has good word about General Sherman."

Men clamored, gathering in a mob in front of Simon and me. "These two boys got nabbed at Kennesaw Mountain, Georgia. They're scouts for Uncle Billy himself."

Simon's trigger-face flashed at Badger. I gazed into the fearful eyes of the sunken faces surrounding me. These men were starving for hope.

"Go ahead," Badger said. "Give the boys some chum. They'll talk plenty for ya." Badger motioned for the crowd to come closer.

An old timer shoved forward from the thick of the crowd and handed two hardtack biscuits into my hands. "What about General Sherman. Is he marching to Atlanta?" The old timer's eyes were watery grey and his hands trembled.

"What about an Exchange?" Another man shoved forward and handed Simon half a cup of brown beans. "Do you know anything at all about an Exchange?"

I didn't know what to say. I turned to Simon. Simon took one of the hardtack biscuits out of my hand and bit into it. "Got any water?" Simon asked the men.

A man handed Simon a canteen. Simon took a cautious smell of the water, and wet his lips.

"It's clean water," the owner of the canteen said.

Simon took a big swig, and said, "Thank you." He passed the canteen to me. "It tastes good, drink up."

"Uncle Billy is near," Simon said.

Badger's grin grew wider. "Is he going to take a battle to Atlanta?"

A silence spread through the men. I drank freely from the canteen, and said, "I betcha one hundred greenbacks he'll take a battle right through the middle of Atlanta!"

The men surged forward. "Have some rice!"

Simon stuffed his beans in his pockets, cupped his palms, and a man poured rice from a tin can into his hands.

"Does Uncle Billy know about the horrors of Andersonville?"

"How long will it take Sherman to reach Sumter County?"

The questions kept coming like shots from a repeating rifle. The better the news we told the men, the more food they showered us with.

Before long the men ran out of food to trade for news, lost interest, and the crowd moved on.

"Come back later!" Badger waved his arms in the air. "They'll be more good news." He turned to us. "Ya boys catch on real fast! Food before honor."

"We got beans, coffee, hardtack," I said.

Simon sat down and sorted through the food the prisoners had given us.

Badger rubbed his scalp and looked up at the sun with a shielding hand. "The sun is going to be blistering hides today. Coffee and hardtack ain't gonna save your fannies from Old Sol. Better get ya some beanpoles fetched up to rig a shebang with."

The warm sunshine on the back of my neck felt good at the moment.

"Hey! Hey! Ya down there with the turnips." Badger staggered away with his horse-hobble legs. "I got something to trade with ya!"

"Great job, boys."

We turned around to see Buckeye.

"Keep up the good work," Buckeye said. "The Tribe can use all that food." Buckeye held open his haversack. "Dump it in here."

We dropped all the food in our hands into Buckeye's sack.

"I'll take what's stuffed in your pockets, too," Buckeye said.

I reached in my pocket and handed Buckeye two hardtack biscuits.

"Hey, Chief. See what the new Indians brought in this morning." Buckeye held the biscuits high above his head.

The big Indian raised his neck up from his scrubbing, nodded, and smiled.

Chief's smile made me feel proud to help the Tribe.

I glanced back over to Chief and saw a man about Father's age handing Chief a dirty shirt. I twisted back around to Buckeye. "Seen any Union officers in here?"

"Only enlisted men here." Buckeye didn't look up from sorting through the food in his haversack.

"There could be officers here," I said.

Simon glared at me.

"It could happen though." I stepped so close to Buckeye I almost stood on his toes. "What if a man wasn't right in the head like Hoosier. What if he was stripped of his uniform, and he didn't even remember he was an officer. He could end up in here, couldn't he?"

Buckeye looked up. "Where are your boots? You better get some cover on your bare socks."

"I lost them," I said. "I'm not worried about my boots. I need to find a Union officer!"

"Lunkhead, what in the heck are you talking about?" Simon squared me up by my shoulders.

I lowered my head. I had thought a lot about Father's medal this morning. *Maybe Father was in the camp and he traded his medal for food? Maybe the Raiders robbed Father too?*

"Cat got your tongue?" Simon prodded my chest with a stiff finger.

"I saw Father's medal."

"You did not!"

"I saw it around that Raider's neck."

"You saw something like his medal."

"I saw bronze — the two inscribed patriots. I even saw the hair-line crack. How many times have we run our fingers over that smooth surface while Father told stories about Grandfather?"

Buckeye stepped closer to me. "Food first. But since you did such a great job of finding food this morning, work on your shebang the rest of today. Don't waste your time looking for anything, besides shelter."

Simon rubbed his face like he was trying to wipe my words away.

"I'll dig a hole for your shebang," Tall Paul said. "You did a fine job of bringing food to the Tribe." He pointed to the coffee that Simon and I traded for sharing fresh news with the old-timers.

"I'd listen to Badger about those beanpoles," Buckeye said.

"We don't have anything worth trading for beanpoles," I said.

"You got your skivvies, don't you?" Buckeye asked.

"Got buttons." I tapped my buttons with my fingertip. "I'm not giving up my skivvies."

"I'd keep the buttons for later, trade the skivvies first,"

Buckeye said.

I moaned.

Buckeye patted my shoulder. "Undergarments are luxuries. Don't believe you boys are in a position to own luxuries."

Simon and I squirmed out of our skivvies. We stored Simon's blanket, our two canteen halves, and two wooden spoons in Hoosier's shebang.

I took my fife with me.

"Skivvies for beanpoles," Simon shouted. "Skivvies for beanpoles." I held my underpants high above my head like a surrender flag as we marched down Main Street.

I felt ridiculous and was very careful where I stepped with my sock feet. I also kept a cautious eye out for Fog Eye. I couldn't let my guard down.

"Got that knife?" I said.

"I've got it." Simon patted his waistband where the knife was well concealed.

"Is it sharp?" I asked.

"Sharp enough to cut your tongue out, Lunkhead. Skivvies! Skivvies!" Simon shouted.

"Why are you mad at me, Simon?"

Simon stopped and lowered his white flag. "I don't believe what you said about Father. Why did you make up something like that?"

"I saw it!"

"Not possible."

"You saying I got poor vision?"

"Don't push me, Will Taylor."

"I'm going to find Father." I stepped carefully over to the closest shebang. "I'll look in every shebang if I have to."

A closed-flap door made out of cornmeal bags covered the entrance to this shebang. I hesitated. The smell of rotting meat was stronger than ever. I held a cupped hand over my nose and mouth, eased the burlap flap back, and peered inside.

"Rats!" I stumbled. Two large rats were gnawing at the peeling flesh of a dead man. I gagged, dropped to my hands and knees, and vomited. Simon patted the back of my neck, squatted down, and lifted my head with a steady hand. "If Father's in here…" he paused and looked me in the eye, "we'll find him."

CHAPTER SIX

Later that afternoon, my waistband rubbed raw below my hipbones. I tugged at the seat of my pants. The material was rough and itchy without skivvies. I had successfully traded my undergarment for two beanpoles. Simon got two beanpoles for his skivvies, too. We staked the poles in the ground where Tall Paul had dug out a cozy den for us. Simon's blue blanket was draped over the top of the poles. It made a good roof.

"Line 'em up!" a coarse Rebel voice called. "Line 'em up, men."

I turned to see a carriage drawn by two old workhorses roll down Main Street. Two gentlemen with wide-brimmed hats and long-tailed coats sat up in the front of the carriage. Their knee-high, leather boots glistened in the sunlight. Captain Wirz sat in the rear next to a dignified woman with a strong chin and unflinching eyes. The woman wore a stiff white dress and a floppy bonnet. A young girl sat next to her. Her dress was identical to the older woman's. Long auburn curls graced her shoulders like a soft silk shawl. Her chin lifted high and her eyes looked straight at us.

Glancing down at my blackened sock feet, I lowered my head. Chief nudged me. "Raise head, Will Taylor."

I quickly looked up. Chief had never spoken my name. I smiled when I saw that Chief stood taller than a Georgia pine.

"Not to be ashamed," said Chief. "Look these people in eyes."

I raised my chin and focused straight at the young girl. She showed no emotion. Her eyes were further out of reach than my freedom.

The horses whinnied and came to a stop right in front of me.

"Blue Bellies look like muddy hogs," one of the aristocratic men said.

Wirz nodded. "Yes, yes. Animals."

The two men up front stood and looked over us prisoners like Generals inspecting their troops.

One of the men took off his hat and cleared his throat. He dabbed sweat from his head with a white handkerchief.

"Time for a stump speech," Badger said.

"Gentlemen, I have word from our president, Jefferson Davis." The man quickened his dabbing.

"He ain't our president," a prisoner yelled.

The other prisoners burst out with laughter.

The man paused and turned to Wirz. Wirz nodded for him to continue.

"President Davis sends word that your government has terminated all exchange of prisoners."

"You're lying!" a prisoner shouted.

A disgruntled moan from the men shivered down the ranks.

The other man in the carriage took off his hat and raised a Bible above his head.

"So help me God, he speaks the truth. Your government has forsaken you." He lowered his Bible over his heart. "We citizens of the Confederate States will not forsake our Northern brothers. We are here today to offer you pardons."

A prisoner belched loud. "Pardon that!"

Laughter roared from the ranks.

Wirz slowly stood, arms crossed tightly over his chest.

"We have good jobs for you," the first man continued. We need cobblers, masons, and blacksmiths for factories in Macon and Savannah. You'll be provided with clean beds, decent clothes, medical care, and most of all, plenty of good cooking."

"How about good-looking women," a prisoner shouted.

"Save your wind for the pulpit, preacher," another prisoner called. "Ain't no traitors in the Union."

Wirz waved his arms in the air. "No rations today! You rude Yankees."

A skeleton of a man stumbled out of the lineup. "You can't starve us to work. We're done starved to death."

The dignified woman stood. "No man will starve. We will help you, but you must at least help yourselves. We need volunteers for the Bake House and the hospital."

"No thanks, Lady. Go back to the plantation and have your slaves do the cooking."

"Quiet! Quiet!" Wirz ordered. "Shut your foul mouths."

The woman gracefully climbed down from the carriage.

All men were quiet.

She pulled the hem of her long dress slightly up so that it didn't touch the ground. She marched within ten feet of the lineup. Her eyes locked on me.

Shifting my feet, I looked away.

"Where are your shoes, son?"

I stared at my toes.

Simon nudged me. "She's talking to you, Lunkhead."

I took a deep breath and closed my eyes.

Simon nudged me harder. "Go on. Don't get us in any trouble."

I stepped forward, stared at the ground, not daring to meet her eyes.

"Speak, child," Wirz said.

"Stolen." I raised my head. "My boots were stolen last night." I leaned to the side and peered around the women at the young girl. She turned her cheek.

"What's your name?" The woman tilted her bonnet to the side and looked at me more closely.

"Will Taylor," I said.

"Come to the Bake House, Will Taylor. I'll see to it that you have boots. Our family brings food and clothes to the Bake House almost every day."

I nodded, did an about-face, and marched back into the lineup. I lowered my head. My right big toe poked out of my blackened sock. I desperately wanted to look at the pretty girl one more time, but I was too ashamed to raise my head.

After the carriage rolled away, Badger slapped my back. "You're in the catbird seat now. You'll be splittin' biscuits with the rich Rebels yet."

"He's not accepting any Johnny Reb hand-me-down boots," Simon said.

"You betcha, he'll take 'em," Buckeye said. "Don't be a stubborn mule, Simon. If he steps on something sharp in here, he'll lose a foot faster than you can say Uncle Billy."

Simon stepped in front of Buckeye. "Taylors aren't traitors."

"Taylors aren't cowards either." I stretched high on my toes, eye level with Simon. "I need those boots. I'm not going to slither around this stockade on my belly like a snake in the grass."

"Those men are out there, Will." Simon took a quick glance over his shoulder. "That one-eyed man will be looking for you."

A lump the size of a chunk of coal stuck in my throat. I tried to swallow hard.

"If he don't want no boots, I'll take 'em," Badger said.

"He needs those boots," Simon said. "I'll go get them for him."

"No," I said. "We both go!"

Later that morning, Buckeye and Chief helped us disguise ourselves as old men in tattered shirts and baggy pants. We hoped the Raiders wouldn't recognize us. Simon and I eased into the bustle of Main Street with our backs hunched.

"Don't think for a minute I didn't see you goggling at that Rebel gal, Lunkhead. The real reason you want to go to the Bake House is to see her."

I raised up. "I wasn't goggling at anybody! And I don't want to see a no-good Rebel girl!"

"Hunch your back." Simon pushed my shoulders lower. "You're going to give us away."

We walked fast, our backs bent and arms swinging like horsetails.

"You looked at her just like you gawked at Becky Adams when she sang her solo in Church."

"I did not!"

"You did, too!"

We got about ten yards shy of the North Gates when a loud commotion erupted like rapid fire from a skirmish line. We stopped, ready to run for the Tribe.

A pack of Raiders were coming our way. To our surprise, the Raiders attacked two new prisoners. The new men had no way to escape. The Raiders had them cornered at the edge of the Deadline. One of the men screamed, "Help! Help us!" The Raiders ripped haversacks from the men, punching, kicking, and clubbing them.

"No one's going to help them," I shouted.

Simon pulled the Arkansas toothpick out.

"No!" I grabbed Simon's sleeve. Simon's trigger-face squinted with fierce intensity.

A shot rang out from a pigeon-roost. The prisoners in the vicinity cheered, "Hooray! Hooray!" One of the Raiders had accidentally rolled under the Deadline. A Rebel boy who couldn't have been more than twelve years old aimed his musket at the other Raiders as they attempted to pull the man who was shot back to the safe side of the line.

"Get back!" The guard steadied his aim at the men. "Get back or I'll shoot you fools. No man crosses the Deadline."

"Let us get our man," one of the Raiders said.

"You cross that line and you'll stay over it for good," the guard shouted.

"Jonas! Jonas!" One of the beaten-up men cried over the top of his battered friend. The Raiders slowly retreated, leaving their shot man behind the Deadline to die.

I eased over to the men the Raiders had attacked. The downed man lay unconscious, his skull cracked open by a club blow. His hair was soaked wet in dark blood. His friend took his own shirt off, and wrapped it tightly around his friend's head.

A steady stream of red poured from the other man's nose.

"Jonas. Speak to me, Jonas."

The other prisoners had all gone back to their business. A bird squawked. A turkey buzzard with widespread wings rested on top of the stockade wall.

Simon picked up a stone and whizzed it at the bird, just missing its head. The buzzard squawked, and lifted into flight. "I hate buzzards!" Simon said.

"That's a sure-shot throwing arm you got there, partner." A tall man stepped forward. Angular and sharp, he looked like human shrapnel. "I'm Jim Bacon. The men call me Quick Jim."

Simon shook his hand. "Simon Taylor. This is my brother Will."

"You boys ever played baseball?"

"What's baseball?" I asked.

Quick Jim laughed. "Where you boys hail from?"

"Kentucky," Simon said.

"Kentucky. I didn't think you were Yankees."

Simon stood taller. "We're Union, that's all that matters."

Quick Jim put a hand on Simon's shoulder. "Come to the Stinks this evening. We've got a baseball game to play. You'll like it. You hit a ball with a stick and run around the field tagging bases."

"What do you tag them with?" I asked.

The man laughed. "Come to the Stinks this evening, you'll see. You better skedaddle from this spot. The Raiders will be back with more men soon. They work the North Gates hard for fresh fish. I'll see to it this injured man gets help."

"Food first," I said as soon as Quick Jim stepped away. "Food first, that's how we survive."

"Don't worry about me, Will. Baseball doesn't sound like much of a game."

When we reached the Bake House, I spotted a pair of boots sitting on the steps. Tied to the laces was a tan tag. It was the same kind of tag that was attached to the big toes of dead men to mark their identity.

I stared at the toe tag. *Was my name on it?*

"Go ahead, Lunkhead." Simon glanced over his shoulder. "Get your Johnny hand-me-down boots and let's get back to the safety of the Tribe."

I slowly picked up one boot and held it where Simon could see a US Army emblem sown into its tongue. "They're not Rebel, they're Union boots."

Simon pulled out his knife, cut the toe tag off, and dropped it on the ground.

I picked up the tag. "That's a dead man's toe tag." I tore it into tiny pieces. "It gives me gooseflesh to see my name on it."

CHAPTER SEVEN

On the way back to the Tribe, we were walking fast with fear of the Raiders being nearby. I slowed down when we passed the prisoner who had been shot earlier for crossing the Deadline. The corpse lay sprawled in the dirt like a toy tossed from the sky. His mouth stretched open in agony.

The sight of the dead man locked my feet up like binding shackles. I couldn't move.

"Lunkhead! Keep up," Simon shouted

I jumped as if the dead man had sat up and grabbed me.

"You're lollygagging!" Simon was fifty paces ahead. He had passed the dead man without a second glance.

I turned to Simon, but couldn't hear a word. Muttering ghost voices from dead men smothered my ears.

Tried to run, but tripped in my new boots, they were too big. I got up quickly, stumbled, and ran to Simon's side.

"What's wrong with you, Will?"

"These boots are too big. They're wobbling on my feet."

Simon grasped my arm and pulled me through the crowd of men. I stumbled, but didn't fall. We weaved, dodged, and bumped our way back to the safety of the Tribe.

Sweating and exhausted, we crawled into our new shebang. Tall Paul had dug us an underground den about seven feet long, five feet wide, and four feet deep. The beanpoles supported the blanket top well. The skivvies were a good trade.

The earthen sidewalls of our shebang felt cool. It was good to be under shelter, even if it did smell like a freshly-dug grave. Outside, the Georgia sun burned steam-engine hot.

The heat slowed the motion and noise of the stockade to a sluggish pace. Only Buckeye's faint voice reading his laundry list to Chief could be heard.

I crawled to the edge of our shebang with my fife, blew two or three practice notes, and played *Lorena* in a slow, mournful tone. Shimmering heat waves rose from the ground like thirsty spirits in search of moisture. *Is Father out there somewhere?*

"He might be out there," I said, not even bothering to look back at Simon in the rear of the shebang. "Father might hear my music," I whispered. "If he hears me, he'll come find me."

Lost deep in the heat, I closed my eyes and drifted back to Kentucky. I pictured the silver-blue grass pastures surrounding our farm. I imagined myself walking down the length of the white fence that stretched for a quarter-mile from the back of the barn to the pond. I could see Father stretched underneath the Sycamore tree with his hat tipped over his eyes. His long locks of red hair looked so distant. The closer I walked, the further Father slipped away. *No, Father, don't leave!*

I opened my eyes and glanced back at Simon. He lay on his back, arms crossed behind his head.

"Simon!"

Simon didn't stir.

"Simon, I know you're awake."

"What? What is it now?"

"Think we'll ever see Kentucky bluegrass again?"

"We'll see it. We'll whip Bobbie Lee and his Rebels yet." Simon sat up. "We're going to escape this place. I know someone in here knows a way out, and we're going to find them."

"What about Father?" I asked.

"Be quiet." Simon scooted closer to the entrance of our shebang. "Where's that singing come from?"

I leaned outside and peered around Simon.

"I don't want no collard greens. All I want's my butter beans!" Badger staggered with heavy horse-legs.

"Badger's drunk again." I ducked back inside.

Badger shook the top of our shebang. "Come on out of ya hole, Simon!"

"You better not tear our roof down!" Simon shouted.

Badger stuck his face inside. His raspy breath smelled like soured turnips. "How about ya boys having a drink with the Badge?"

Simon lunged at him. "Get out of here, you stink!" Badger stumbled backwards, fell flat on his rump, turned his bottle up, and took a big gulp. "I don't want no collard greens. All I want's my butter beans." He belched. "Hey Willy boy. Heared ya got new boots. Come on out and let me see 'em."

"Let's go on out there, so he'll shut up," I said. Outside the shebang, I flopped my feet around like a newborn colt. The boots were at least two sizes too big.

Badger laughed at me. "Ya look like a circus clown," he said. He reached in his pocket, and pulled out a shriveled tomato. "Here's a red nose for ya!"

"Leave him alone," Tall Paul said. He stepped closer to me, and looked up at the guards on the parapet. "Take your boots off."

I trusted Tall Paul. My big boots slipped off easily. I didn't even have to untie them. Tall Paul reached into his pockets, and pulled out a fist full of red dirt. He packed the dirt inside my boots.

"This will keep them from sliding," Tall Paul said. "It's good, soft clay."

I thought it was odd, but didn't protest. I put my boots back on and walked in a tight circle. Within a minute, the clay formed around my toes and stopped the sliding.

"It works," I said. "Thanks."

"All this dirt is good for something," Tall Paul said. He dumped a mess of rice, beans, and bacon into the stew brewing in his kettle. Buckeye blew on the embers of a struggling campfire.

Badger finished off his bottle with one big gulp, and tossed it on the ground. He sang, "I wish I weren't in the land of cotton, where these Rebs weren't so rotten. Look away, look away, look away, Dixie boys." He kicked his empty bottle over to Hoosier. "Hey Hoosier. Ya givin' Leroy and Lola a bath?"

Hoosier sat crossed-legged with half a wooden canteen in front of him filled with brown water. Ignoring Badger, he pushed a tiny floating, cupped leaf around with the tip of a twig.

"Let's see 'em." Badger stumbled over. He tripped, and bumped Hoosier. Water splashed from the dish.

"Lola's overboard!" Hoosier cried. "She can't swim!"

"Agh, she's all right. I can see her," Badger slurred.

"Lola! Lola!" Hoosier screamed. "Help!"

Badger grabbed for the dish and knocked it over. The water soaked into the thirsty ground.

"Lola! Leroy!" Hoosier lowered his face. Tears streamed his dirty cheeks.

Chief snatched Badger by the back of his shirt and jerked

his feet right off the ground. "Easy, Chief," Badger said. "Easy big feller." He pulled his knees up to his chest to avoid being dragged through the campfire. Chief tossed him into the center of Main Street.

Badger slunk away like a scolded dog.

Chief picked up a dirty shirt and vigorously scrubbed.

Hoosier sobbed.

"Hate like the Devil to see Hoosier like this," Buckeye said. "Badger don't know when to stop. Can't help it. Whiskey's got the best of him."

Tall Paul lifted a wooden ladle to his lips and tasted his stew. I tried to help Hoosier find Lola and Leroy. Hoosier insisted they were lost at sea.

The mood at supper was somber with hardly a word spoken. Chief didn't ask me to play my fife. Everyone went into their shebangs when the food was gone.

"Hooray! Hooray!" We hadn't been inside our shebang very long when the sound of cheering men came from the direction of the Stinks.

Simon scurried to the entrance. "Hey, we forgot to find Quick Jim's baseball game. Let's go to the Stinks!"

"I thought you said earlier that baseball didn't sound like much of a game to you," I said.

"I did," Simon said. "I just want to see those men making fools of themselves."

We walked quickly to the Stinks. I was surprised to see a crowd of rowdy men jumping up and down with raised arms shouting and cheering. "Hit it where they ain't," a man shouted.

Quick Jim smashed a white ball with a stick. A man tried to catch it with his bare hands. He bobbled the ball and dropped it.

"Hooray!" the crowd cheered. Quick Jim scrambled across the field, his long arms and legs swinging wildly like a white-tail deer dodging tight trees.

"They're playing Four O'Cat with nine men," Simon said. "Baseball's just like Four O'Cat." He stood on his toes watching Quick Jim round the bases. "It's no different than what we play in Kentucky. There's just more men. I can play this game with the best of these players."

"Hooray!" the men shouted and clapped when Quick Jim made it back to the spot where he had first hit the ball.

"New York Volunteer Infantry, five, Zouaves, four," an old man said. He scribbled numbers on a ledger.

A creepy feeling pricked at the back of my neck. I twisted around as if a big animal were stalking me from the edge of the crowd. I scanned the faces of men for Fog Eye. All the dirty men looked alike. Their faces looked like wide mouths and squinty eyes that had been painted on blackened cooking pots.

"Put it here pitcher!" a new batter shouted. "Right down the middle. That's where I like it. I'll knock the tar out of it!"

The ball swooshed down the middle and the batter whirled around with a wild swing.

"Strike!"

"Foul," the batter shouted. "That was outside!"

The men laughed.

"Let's go, Simon," I said, and tugged on his sleeve. "Let's get back to the Tribe."

"It's just getting fun," Simon replied.

I pulled harder on his sleeve. "I've got a feeling something bad is going to happen."

Simon glared at me. "Whats is it? What do you see?"

"I don't see anything," I said. "That's the problem. I can't see them, but I just know there's someone watching me."

Later that night, inside our shebang, I pulled my shirt off and wrapped it around my fife to make a pillow. Something itched under my armpit; I pinched around, and found my first Grayback. *Was it Leroy or Lola?* I considered taking it to Hoosier, but flicked it outside instead.

I left my boots on and tied the strings together in a tight knot to make sure no one stole them during the night. Simon fell right asleep on the dirt floor. I couldn't rest; I had too much on my mind. Murky images of Fog Eye and Father swished behind my eyelids.

"Post number ten, here's your mule, all's well," a young guard's voice called from a nearby pigeon-roost.

"Post eleven, clock struck nine, all's well," a more distant, old man's voice called.

Sentry voices faded down the parapet as light as a thin mist until they could no longer be heard. The train whistle from Anderson Station howled. "Coming or going?" I asked myself in a whisper. Sickening moans and cries came from neighboring shebangs. Vicious tracking dogs barked from the direction of the Dead House. *Was Father escaping? No, Father, wait for me!*

Sinking. I could feel myself sinking deep into the sleepy depths of a dream. I could see the steep, jagged, shimmering rocks of Missionary Ridge protruding from the earth. The mountain swayed like rolling waves. "It's crashing. The mountainside is crashing." I glanced behind me for an escape route. The hungry ground collapsed all around me like a giant mouth trying to swallow. "Run! Run!" I sucked at my lips like a last death breath and ran to the banks of the river. The water was blood red: boulders, trees, and mud roared like a thousand rumbling cannons.

The only way to escape was to cross the river of blood. I

heard my name called from the opposite bank. On the other side I could see Father. A girl was with him. They both waved for me to jump into the blood. I squinted hard and could see that it was the girl with auburn hair.

I screamed, "No!" and sat straight up. I was now wide-awake. Rapid-fire heartbeats rattled the inside of my bones.

"What's wrong?" Simon asked.

I didn't answer. I cocked my head to hear thunder grumble far off in the Georgia fields. The first splattering raindrops hit the top of the blanket.

"It's raining," I said. Simon scurried around and found our canteen halves. He quickly placed them outside to collect drinking water for the morning. I crawled outside, tilted my head back and opened my mouth wide. I licked raindrops from my lips. The salt and moisture tasted good. I wanted to stand outside in the rain all night, but Simon made me come back inside the shebang. I was too tired to argue with him. I crawled close to Simon, lay down, and tightly closed my eyes. I hoped that the Auburn-hair girl would return in a better dream. I wondered if I volunteered for Bake House duty, would I see her again?

CHAPTER EIGHT

Next morning Badger rejoined the Tribe. He sheepishly loaded his pockets for another day of trading. It was the first time I had seen him somber and quiet. *Where did he find a safe place to sleep last night?* The scent of fresh rainwater saturated everything in camp. The stink was even washed clean for the moment. Tall Paul and Buckeye were busy wringing every drop of clean water they could get out of Chief's laundry into the kettle. Chief stood in a mud puddle over his washtub scrubbing and scrubbing a pair of ragged trousers.

Hoosier talked peacefully inside his shebang. *Did this mean Leroy and Lola were now safe?*

The morning sun heated the moisture like a simmering soup of humidity. Suddenly, a boisterous group of men scurried down Main Street. They pursued a dozen swooping birds that were zooming in and out of a swarm of tiny black flies. The prisoners chased after the birds hurling shoes, canteens, and tin cups.

"Fresh bird meat!" Simon struggled to pull off one of his boots. I knew that if anyone could knock a bird from the sky, Simon could. I had once seen Simon pop a crow off the top of a fence-rail with a stone from more than thirty feet away.

"Get us a bird!" I waved my arms. "Get us a bird, Simon!"

Men were slipping and sliding, splashing and sloshing in the puddles. One boy, not much older than me, knocked a bird from the air with an iron skillet. The boy sat down and took a savage bite from the bird.

My stomach churned at the sight of blood and feathers.

Simon's boot was too heavy and bulky. He couldn't throw it straight enough to hit a fast-moving bird. It fell short every throw. Frustrated, Simon pulled his sock off, stuffed the Arkansas toothpick inside, and crouched down waiting for just the right moment. When the birds turned around and passed back by him, he sprung up, slung the sock around the top of his head like a lasso, and let it go. The weapon shot through the air with projectile accuracy, feathers exploded upon the impact.

"Hooray!" I jumped up and down. "Hooray!" I paused, and hoped that Simon would not eat the bird raw.

Quick Jim ran up. "I saw it! I saw it all. You hit that bird like a sharpshooter! We've got to have you on our baseball team."

Simon held the dead bird gently in his cupped palms. "All I'm doing is cooking this bird."

"Food first," I said to Quick Jim. "We've got to go!"

Simon and I started walking toward our shebang. I glanced behind me. Quick Jim was following us. His face gleamed. His angular elbows swung like wheat sickles.

We stopped walking just shy of our shebang when Simon found a broken beanpole on the ground. He picked it up and stuck the dead bird onto its splintered tip. "Not much meat," he said. He rotated the bird on the stick like he was practicing cooking it over a campfire.

"Let me teach you how to pitch," Quick Jim said.

Simon looked up with raised brows. "Huh?"

Quick Jim reared back and threw an invisible ball. "It's easy to sling a baseball."

Buckeye gaited over from where he had been writing in his ledger. "Food first, Simon!"

"I told him that already," I said.

"There's plenty of food for the winners." Quick Jim puffed his chest out. "That's the wager. Winners get half of the losers' daily rations."

"You're not too plump yourself." Simon eyed Jim's skinny bones from forehead to toes. "Maybe I ought to play for the other team."

Quick Jim chuckled. "That's why we need you to volunteer for our team." He slapped his protruding ribs. "So we can all fatten up like Christmas chickens."

"I'm volunteering for rations duty at the Bake House," I said. "I've been thinking this over all day."

"Hooray for Will Taylor." Buckeye slapped my back.

Simon wedged himself between Buckeye and me. "He's not going anywhere without me. And I'm not helping any Rebels."

"Wait just a cotton pickin' minute." Buckeye thumped Simon on his chest with a cocked thumb. "That's the best way to help the Tribe." Buckeye reached out and pulled me closer to him, and put his one arm over my shoulder. "He can swindle out of the Bake House salt, pepper, potatoes, hardtack, coffee, you name it."

"We don't want to help the Rebels do any kind of work," Simon said, and pushed me a step away. "What if he gets caught stealing?"

Buckeye reached far out, patted my head. "He's clever, he won't get caught."

"He's right, Simon," Quick Jim said. "You boys can't survive on tiny birds alone."

Simon looked at the brittle bird bones, then back at me.

Now, high on my tiptoes, I peered out into the distance.

"Lunkhead," Simon said. "You seeing a ghost? Why are you pale all of a sudden?"

"Father!" I pointed. "There, in the center of those men across the street. See his red hair?"

"Where?" Simon craned his neck. "I don't see him."

"You're not talking me out of it!" I pushed off of Simon and ran away.

Simon chased after me.

"Father!" I tugged at the back of the man's shirt.

The man spun around. His cheeks were scarred with deep, scabby pockmarks. I stumbled back, now relieved this face wasn't Father's.

"What?" the man said. "What is it you want?"

Not a word came out of my open mouth. The man glared, and said, "You don't want me, boy."

"He's not here, Will." Simon's voice was soothing. He squeezed the back of my neck with his strong fingers.

"He's here somewhere." I lowered my head. "I know he's here. I saw his medal."

Simon raised my head, smudged a tear away from my cheek with a knuckle. "You're wasting water. Better not let Chief see you waste water."

"What if Father is in here?" I peered back at the man with the scarred face. "What if he escapes without us?"

"Okay, Will, if you'll shut up about it, I'll do the searching while you're at the Bake House."

"You go, Will Taylor." Chief stopped scrubbing and slightly nodded his chin toward my direction.

I walked over to Chief and extended my fife to him. "Keep my fife safe for me while I'm gone Chief."

Chief nodded, took the fife, and hid it under a pile of shirts.

I turned to face Simon. "Badger was wrong about me, Simon. I'm going to make it. I'm going to survive this place!"

On the way to the Bake House, I could see the silhouettes of men going about their business from the corners of my eyes. I edged closer to Simon and constantly tugged at my trousers. I would rather have my skivvies back than new boots.

I looked down, and noticed that the tips of my new boots were too shiny. I could see men enviously eyeing my feet. I lowered my head and dragged my toes, scuffing my boot tips as I walked behind Simon.

Suddenly Simon stopped; I bumped right into him.

"Here he comes!" Simon clutched my arm. "You listen to what I tell you. No back talk!"

Not more than twenty paces away, Fog Eye and two other Raiders were closing in on us.

"We've got to run!" I tugged at Simon's sleeve.

Simon whipped the Arkansas toothpick out. "You run, don't talk back!" Simon shoved me. "Run like a hare to the Bake House, now!"

My legs wobbled as I tried to run. The big boots clumsily clomped. I zig-zagged through a group of tightly-spaced shebangs. When I knew I was well hidden behind a tall, teepee-shaped shebang, I stopped, and poked my head up.

"He's a lunatic," I said to myself. Simon was walking head-on into the Raiders.

About five paces from them, Simon shouted, "Go milk your

goats with your nose!" He dashed away from Main Street and ran between the shebangs. The Raiders chased him. I knew they couldn't catch Simon. He was swift as a fox.

I ducked down behind a tall shebang. When I was sure it was safe, I rose up, and tried to spot Father's medal tied around Fog Eye's neck, but the distance was too great to see it. Simon had vanished from sight, too; I turned and dashed for the Bake House.

Out of breath and dripping with sweat, I stepped onto the rickety porch. The Bake House was a square building, not much bigger than a sharecropper's shack. It sat very near an open gate where a supply wagon was leaving the prison. *Was there a way to hide in a supply wagon?*

Before I could think another thought, a guard grabbed my sleeve and ushered me inside the Bake House. The Rebels put me straight to work helping quarter a full wagonload of potatoes. I sat on a long workbench and had to cut each potato in half, then halve each piece with a knife that wasn't fit to slice butter.

The potatoes were dusty and caked with clumps of dirt. The raw scent of earth made me think of fresh graves. I surveyed the backside of the Bake House cautiously for a way out, but there was only a front door, and no windows.

All morning long I worried about Simon. *Was Simon okay? How would he get back to the Tribe safely? How would he find Father?*

By midday I had a headache from thinking too hard and my palms ached right where the thumb joins the hand from cutting nearly one hundred potatoes. While massaging my sore thumbs, I closely observed the other men working. Most of them were commandeered slaves. They kept to themselves humming *Amazing Grace*, occasionally chatting with one another in soft voices.

There were also a few older Union prisoners. None of the men even glanced at me, much less talked to me. They kept their heads down most of the time. I thought that these men looked too old to fight. Their hands were wrinkled and caked with dirt as if they had been digging their own graves. I looked at my young hands, and had to chuckle. I was a fifer too young to fight.

As the day went on, I noticed that one slave smiled at me from time to time with jerky glances. When none of the Rebels were nearby, the slave eased close to me. He was a stocky man, his head as round as a pumpkin. His neck was compact, close to his shoulders. A twitch in his neck made his chin jerk back and forth. His wide back looked stout enough to tote cannons.

"Lamar," the man whispered.

I smiled. "Will. My name is Will Taylor." He shook my hand. Lamar's grip trembled, but was as hard to squeeze as iron.

Lamar handed me a new potato, nodded, and retreated to a far corner.

Later in the day, when the sun had been high in the sky for hours, I knew why they called it the Bake House. It was hot as an oven inside. I felt like I had been dipped in a river. Round drops of sweat blotted my forehead like dewdrops. My neck bobbed sleepily up and down.

I then dropped a perfectly round potato. It thumped across the warped floor, thudded against a wall, and disappeared down a gap between floorboards.

The guard stepped over. "You dropped that on purpose, now you're going to fetch it!"

Lamar stepped over, knelt down, and peered into the dark hole. "Don't see a thing." He tried to reach inside the hole, but his arm was too thick to fit.

"Reach down and find it!" The guard banged his rifle butt

on the floor.

"Let me try," I said. I crouched and stuck my arm down the hole. I reached around, touching nothing but cool dirt. "It's gone."

"You're gonna have to crawl under the Bake House," the guard said. "There's rats under there, big as polecats."

I felt my heart beat faster.

"I'll fetch it," Lamar said.

"You're too big to fit under there," I said. I wedged between Lamar and the guard. "I did it, I'll get it."

Outside with the guard, I dropped to my hands and knees, and poked my head under the Bake House floor. *Snakes, spiders, anything but rats,* I thought.

The guard nudged me in the rear with a boot heel. "Get moving!"

I crawled forward. My back touched some sagging floorboards. Footsteps clomped above my head. I flattened out on my stomach as flat as a snake and scooted deep under the house.

At the far end of the building, dust flittered in the sunlight. *Was it a small gap to freedom?*

"Get moving under there!" the guard ordered.

A tap, tap, tap noise came from the floor above, and someone hummed *Amazing Grace.* A lot of dust fell from this area. *Someone's marking the spot for me where the potato fell through the hole.*

I moved toward the humming and tapping, and swept along the floor with my right arm. I pulled myself forward with my left arm. Finally, the tip of my fingers poked the potato, and it rolled. When I got a firm grip on it, I tapped back on the floor above my head. The tapping from above stopped.

"Find it?" the Rebel called out.

I hesitated, and yelled, "Not yet!"

Out of the corner of my eye, I saw a small shadow move. I froze stiff as a day-old corpse. I slowed my breathing and listened. The shadow squeaked closer with black, beady eyes and a lifted nose. I ducked back. A rat passed right by me.

I kept my eye on the retreating tail switching back and forth, and strained my neck to see it disappear down a huge hole about the size of a wagon wheel. *That was no rat hole.*

"Whatcha doing under there?" the guard shouted.

"I see it, I see it," I called back. I squirmed closer to the hole, feeling damp, loose dirt. When I reached the opening, the dirt was packed firm. "I'll be, a man-made hole," I said.

I reached into it and felt around. No loose dirt. Wood splints braced the sides. A tunnel!

"Get on out from under there!" The guard banged his rifle butt against the side of the building.

"I've got it," I yelled back. "I've got it."

I crawled back out with my prize find.

Later that day, I pilfered around the Bake House, and found coffee, small potatoes, and beans. While the guards were talking, I emptied the clay from my boots and dumped it down the hole where the potato had fallen. The extra space in my boots made for a perfect hiding place for food. I was proud to help the Tribe. I couldn't wait to show Simon the food, and tell him about the secret tunnel. I knew Simon would want to see the escape tunnel right away. We would have to be very careful.

CHAPTER NINE

At dusk, the guards escorted all of us workers outside the Bake House. Lamar and I were the last two outside. I sucked in fresh air, feeling my chest rise. Potato dust covered me from head to toe. I sighed in relief when I saw that Simon stood with Tall Paul and Buckeye about twenty paces from the rickety porch.

"Simon!" I ran fast toward my brother. I slowed a step when the food in my boots squished between toes.

"What did you find out?" I asked, before I even reached Simon's side.

Simon glared. "About what?"

"About Father. You said you would look for him today."

"Let's get moving, boys, while the road's still clear," Buckeye said, nervously looking around for Raiders.

"I'll tell you back at the Tribe," Simon said.

"Tell me what?" I stood on my toes and leaned closer to Simon's eyes.

"Get marching, boys!" Buckeye ordered. "We don't want to get jumped out here in the open!"

Simon grabbed my sleeve. "I've got a lot to tell you!"

"I've got a lot to tell you, too." I twisted my neck and checked behind me. Lamar vanished like a shadow in the shade.

We swiftly made it back to the safety of the Tribe. Badger sat beside the cooking kettle eating a raw turnip. An empty bottle lay at his feet. "How's the Bake House, Willy boy?"

I shrugged, and turned away.

"Did ya eat butter beans with Captain Wirz?"

"Shut up, Badger," Simon said.

Badger jumped up. He wobbled, laughed, and kicked his empty bottle. "I don't want no collard greens, all I want's my butter beans. See that girl standing thar, she's not as pregnant as she seems, she's just full of butter beans," Badger sang.

"Shut that awful singing up," Buckeye said.

Badger stretched his skinny neck high trying to project his voice even louder. "Turnip sandwich a delight, bread 'n butter is all right. Pass the cornbread if ya please and another bowl of them good 'ole butter beans..."

"Don't you know any songs other than Butter Beans?" Buckeye snapped.

"I know none of your biz-wax, cornbread, and shoe-tacks, yackety, yack, yack, yack," Badger said. "Want to hear that?"

"No thanks," Buckeye answered.

Badger waltzed a little dance over to me and swayed back and forth like he was on the deck of a rolling ship. His sour breath smelled like spoiled pickles. I sidestepped away and sat on the ground next to Hoosier, who was sitting quietly by the campfire.

I untied my boots and emptied my stash next to Tall Paul's kettle. Out came a handful of coffee and a baker's dozen of beans. Then, four small potatoes no bigger than hen eggs rolled out of my outturned pockets. That's all I dared to sneak out on my first day on the job.

Chief smiled and handed me my fife. I felt proud and grinned wide.

"By cracky. Look what the little fox done got out of the Bake House." Badger slapped my back.

"Boy's not gonna outdo the Badge." He staggered over to his shebang and came back out with cupped palms full of food. "Rally around the flag, boys! I got hardtacks, turnips, onions, salt pork, and don't forget who brought the Pine-Top." He laughed and dumped all the food right on the ground next to the kettle. "Shindig tonight!" He bumped Hoosier.

"Watch out!" Hoosier shouted.

Hoosier wobbled on the ground with Indian-style crossed legs. He turned his back on Badger, and continued to talk with his chin down, poking his index finger inside his front pocket.

"Hoosier," Badger said. "That Leroy and Lola ya talking to in your pocket?"

Hoosier scooted further away. Chief grunted at Badger. Badger shook his head, and took another big drink from his bottle of Pine-Top. "Boys, I do believe this Pine-Top whisky is making my teeth fall out." He spit a yellow tooth on the ground, and rubbed a finger over his bleeding gums.

I leaned over close to Simon and whispered, "Any sign of Father?"

Simon frowned and picked dirt from his nails. "Nothing. Not a track."

"Why are your hands so dirty?" I asked.

Simon shrugged, wiping his hands on his thighs. Particles of red clay were caked to his trousers. His face and neck were powdered with dust.

"You been digging, haven't you?" I asked.

Simon flashed his trigger-face. "We're clearing a field." He glanced over his shoulder. "A field for playing baseball. No digging."

I knew better than to ask any more questions. I wanted to tell Simon about the tunnel I had found under the Bake House, but I could see that Badger cocked his head as if he were trying hard to listen.

My secret would have to stay safe in my head for now. I knew that Simon had a secret, too. *He must be in on digging a tunnel*, I thought. *What if the guards catch him? The penalty could be death. Maybe Simon's tunnel connected with the one under the Bake House?* I rubbed my temples. I had so many questions that my brain throbbed. I would have to wait until after supper to talk with Simon in private.

We had a feast, but not a shindig that night. There was really nothing to celebrate. Still it was the most food I had eaten in months. I felt like I had swallowed a ten-pound cannonball.

Near the end of our super, Badger guzzled down the bottle of Pine-Top and tossed the empty container beyond the Deadline. It landed with a clank, but didn't break.

"What a waste," I said. "Could have used that bottle for a water container."

A loud shot suddenly rang out. I ducked when I felt pieces of glass scatter over the top of my head.

Badger laughed and danced around the campfire slapping his knees. "Did ya see that shot? Did ya see that shot, boys?"

The shot set off something in Hoosier. "Leroy, Lola! They're lost!" He crawled around on his hands and knees.

Badger tossed a stone a few feet from the shebangs. "Over there." He pointed and snickered.

Hoosier stood and stumbled. He was stooped-over with his head down. His hands were cupped around the sides of his eyes like he was desperately searching for something on the ground.

Chief growled and turned to face Badger. Badger slithered into a fringe of darkness beyond our shebangs like a timid dog.

"Hoosier!" Buckeye shouted. "Get away from there!"

"Leroy!" Hoosier, cried. "Lola!"

He tripped, and rolled right under the wood railing that marked the Deadline.

I jumped up and ran for Hoosier. Within two steps, Simon knocked me to the ground with a hard shove.

A second musket shot silenced the night.

"No!" I cried. "You didn't warn him. It's not right. You didn't even warn him!"

Hoosier lay motionless, face down beyond the Deadline.

Simon held me down. The guards up in the pigeon-roost said nothing. The skinny round tips of black musket barrels aimed right at us.

"Back inside our shebangs, boys," Buckeye said. "There's nothing we can do for him now."

Tall Paul, Buckeye, Simon and I all entered our shebangs. I looked back to see Chief as stiff and silent as a totem pole.

"Simon, I found a way out," I whispered.

Simon signaled for me to crawl to the center of our dugout. We were now as far as we could get from our walls and door. "We're digging a tunnel," Simon said.

"I know," I said.

Simon grabbed my arm tight. "No one's supposed to know. Who told you?"

"I found it on my own."

"Not possible." Simon stiffened up as if he were sitting in a church pew. "You don't know where our tunnel is!"

"I do too! It's under the Bake House."

"You keep your mouth shut, Lunkhead. Stay away from that tunnel. And don't let Badger know about anything. Don't trust him."

"I won't. I promise." I leaned closer to him. "We've got to find Father, soon."

"He's not here, Will."

"You haven't looked!"

"I did. I searched around some today."

"You can't search some. You have to search a lot!" I vigorously rubbed my forehead, tying to wipe my mind free. "You keep digging, I'll look for Father," I said.

"Listen to me, Will. You've got to go back to the Bake House, that's your part now. We have a plan. We've got a lot of ground to cover once we're in the woods. We need all the food you can get. There's a whole mess of people working on this escape. They call themselves the Underground Railroad. Slaves, and even sympathetic Rebs on the outside are helping us."

"I know we can find him," I said. "You have to keep searching."

Simon placed his open palms on my cheeks and looked me in the eye, just the way Father did when he was trying to make a point with one of us. "We've got three more days of digging," Simon said. "Quick Jim and the boys from Tennessee say three more days of filling our boots and pockets with that Hellish red clay. We carry the dirt to the Stinks and dump it in the water by the baseball field." He shook his head, frowning. "Wish we could have gotten Hoosier out. Three more days, that's all he needed."

I nodded, grabbed my fife, and crawled to the front of the shebang. I wished I could cry for Hoosier, but my tears were as dry as potato dust.

The camp was lifeless this night. Not a man stirred. The lonely train whistle howled in the distance. I placed my lips to my fife, and blew a long note that sounded like a lost loon on a foggy lake. *Three more days. Father will hear my music. Wherever he is, he'll hear my music, and know that it's me.*

Clickity-clack, clickity-clack. I opened my eyes and shook from a chill. My hair was wet with dew from falling asleep at the entrance of our shebang. I quickly found my fife. *Clickity-clack, clickity-clack.* Blinking, rubbing my eyes, I strained to see in the darkness. The noise came from Chief's shebang.

I crawled out of our shelter. *Clickity-clack, clickity-clack.* Underneath the strange noise, I could now hear a low sobbing moan. I cautiously peered through the darkness. I could see Chief's hunched-over shadow, furiously scrubbing. My vision adjusted and I could see a pale body. Hoosier's stripped corpse lay on the ground beside Chief's washtub.

Far in an Eastern sky, a bright morning star was rising. "Where are you Father?" I whispered to the star. "Where are you?"

A slight breeze blew through camp. All sounds stopped. I stood silent, staring over at Chief's shadow. His long arms were raised. He chanted an eerie animal sound. I shivered. I didn't want Chief to see me. I crouched down low and softly stepped back to my shebang.

CHAPTER TEN

Morning sun warmed the eastern side of the shebang. I opened my eyes to flat streams of slicing sunlight. Mules snorted nearby. Men hummed a hymn. Simon was already outside. I poked my head out, and cringed from a whiff of rotting meat smell. The Dead Wagon had arrived. Two slave teamsters mournfully harmonized a soft hymn. Chief walked to the wagon with Hoosier draped in his arms like a sleeping bride. Hoosier's clothes were wet, but clean. Chief placed the body on top of the other corpses. He folded Hoosier's arms across his chest.

Buckeye strolled over, and parted Hoosier's hair with a comb. Tall Paul reached up under his shirt, plucked two lice out, and stuck them in Hoosier's front pocket. "Don't forget Leroy and Lola."

Simon stood silent at the side of the wagon with his head lowered. Badger was nowhere to be found. The lonely train whistle howled her beckoning call.

"Goodbye, Hoosier," I said. I lifted my fife to my lips, and played *Yankee Doodle Dandy.*

"Yankee Doodle went to town, riding on a pony," Simon sang. "Stuffed a feather in his cap..."

The mules clomped away. My notes faded, and Simon stopped singing. The wagon wasn't even out of sight, before Chief started scrubbing again.

"Time to get to work," Tall Paul said.

"The work goes on," Buckeye added.

Simon looked me right in the eye. "Time for the Taylors to get to work!"

"I know what I have to do," I said.

"Quick Jim and three or four of his men will be here soon," Simon said. "We'll see you safely to the Bake House."

"Simon." I tightly squeezed his arm. "Don't stop looking."

"I'll look," Simon said. "I'll look when I can."

When I reached the Bake House, Lamar was unloading sacks of cornmeal from the back of a long, black horse carriage. Just when I stepped onto the rickety porch, I heard the voices of women inside the Bake House. I lowered my head, glanced at the tips of my scuffed-up boots. I was glad my dirty toes weren't poking out from sock holes. It was good to have boots covering my bare feet, but I was as dirty as a gravedigger.

"Good morning, Will Taylor."

Surprised, I quickly looked up to see the pretty girl with the auburn hair, and her mother.

I lifted my chin as high as I could. "Morning," I mumbled and tried to stare straight ahead. I couldn't help from peeking out from the corner of my eye.

The girl smiled, lifted her chin, raised the hem of her dress, and stepped into the carriage. Her black shoes were as polished as a General's riding boots. I wanted to look behind me, but forced myself forward.

Inside the Bake House, I went right to work crushing up cornmeal. Sometime around mid-morning, when the guards were on the front porch chatting, I eased over to Lamar.

"What's her name?

Lamar smiled. "Susanna Wilcox."

"She's beautiful," I said.

"And as clever as an old coon." Lamar craned his neck to make sure the guards weren't watching. "Master Wilcox's my owner."

I had only been back to work for a few minutes when I heard a familiar voice outside the Bake House wall.

"By cracky, Captain…"

Badger? What's Badger doing out here? I inched closer, flattened my body to the wall, and peered out a wormhole in a splintered wallboard.

Badger and Wirz stood close together. Badger chomped down on a fat cigar that was identical to the cigar Wirz was smoking.

"Damn Yankees," Wirz said. "I'll hang the lot of them." He whirled around, marched toward the Guardhouse, uttering a string of muffled words. Badger chased after him. "Captain, Captain, where's my pay?"

I turned. Lamar was standing right next to me, his head twitching back and forth.

"Lamar," I said, "Do you know Badger?"

At that moment, a guard poked his head inside the Bake House. "Get to work!" he shouted. "You two want a whip slashing?"

Lamar turned his back on the guard, lowered his head, and walked across the room.

I glared at the guard.

"What you looking at?" The guard stepped forward.

I shook my head in silence, sat down on my workbench, and got busy crushing cornmeal. I couldn't stop thinking about Badger. *Why did he ask for pay? What did Badger tell Captain Wirz?*

Within forty-five minutes, there was a loud commotion outside the Bake House. All the guards were still outside. I shoved my way past three slaves and two old prisoners blocking the doorway and stepped outside on the porch.

Wirz was on horseback. He had a detail of a dozen musket-armed Rebels and tracking dogs. "Present arms!" Wirz ordered. "Fire at will on any prisoner attempting to escape."

A thought thumped me like a bird flopping into the side of my head. *"Badger...Badger's a traitor."* I slouched my shoulders and leaned against the wall.

"Back in the Bake House!" A guard fanned his musket barrel. I stepped inside, and instantly saw the hole in the floorboards. *If only I could get under the Bake House, I could escape through the tunnel and warn Simon.*

"I dropped a potato down that hole," I said, leaning outside of the doorframe. "I'll go get it!"

The guard glared at me. "No one's to leave the Bake House. Captain's orders." He closed the front door tight.

I ran to the hole, grabbed the edge of the board, and pulled with all my might. If I could only break a board loose, I could crawl under the house. My sharp breaths burned.

A strong hand grabbed my arm and pulled me up. It was Lamar.

"I've got to warn Simon, Lamar!"

"Look at this." Lamar pulled his shirt off, and turned his back to me. "You don't want a thrashing."

Strips of scar tissue as wide as a belt criss-crossed his back.

Lamar's head twitched. He reached up, held his hands to his cheeks like he might stop his face twitching.

I pressed my back against the wall, slid down, and pulled my legs tight to my chest. I couldn't do anything at the moment but try to hold myself together. All the men in the Bake House worked in silence. In the distance, dogs barked, men shouted, and gunfire rattled.

I ran to the door when I heard horses and dogs outside the Bake House. Wirz stopped his horse and looked right at me. "Caught the men digging a tunnel. One boy's dead and two are going to the Stocks. Let this be a lesson for all of you. No attempts to escape!"

The words "One boy's dead," pierced through my side like a bayonet. *Was it Simon?*

I spent the remainder of the day chopping up potatoes. I couldn't sit still for more than a few minutes at a time. I paced around the Bake House in an endless circle of worry. I needed to know Simon was all right.

Lamar tried his best to comfort me with encouraging whispers, but his words drifted through my mind without sticking one bit.

Late that evening, when the guards opened the Bake House door, I rushed onto the porch. No sign of Simon. I swallowed a deep breath, sighed, and felt emptiness sink into my chest. I lowered my head, but snapped my neck right up when I remembered Chief's words: *"Raise head, Will!"* I turned around to see Lamar standing in the doorway of the Bake House. "I've got to find Simon!"

"I'll help you," Lamar said.

Lamar and two of his friends walked with me down Main Street. We weren't far from our camp when a rowdy group of men tumbled out into the center of Main. The men seemed to be split into two distinct groups. They pushed, postured, and shouted. Soon punches flew and the group was all balled up in a gigantic mass rolling back and forth across the street.

The men soon tired, and the dust settled. The two groups slowly rose. Both sides paused for a few seconds, not sure what to do next.

"Charge!" a man shouted. "Let's whip these Raiders." The punches started flying again. Arms and legs flailed in chaos.

An old man grabbed my arm and handed me an iron skillet. "Let's get 'em, boy! We're whopping the Raiders."

I gasped as the man slammed his old body into the action.

Fog Eye stumbled from the pile of men. He looked right at me with his one good eye. I ducked behind Lamar. "That's him!" I peered around and spotted the medal dangling from Fog Eye's neck. "He's got Father's medal!"

"There's that hooligan from New York," a man with a club shouted. "Get him! He's the one who killed Ben Wheeler!"

Fog Eye fled into the thickness of the shebangs. A group of men with clubs pursued him. "The medal!" I shouted. "I've got to get it!"

I raised the skillet above my head and yelled, "Hooray! Let's whip the Raiders!" I took five long strides in the direction of the men chasing Fog Eye, but Lamar caught me by the seat of my baggy pants.

"Your brother," Lamar said. "You've got to find your brother."

The words stopped me like a lasso of reason noosed around my neck. I pivoted with hesitation.

Fog Eye was already out of sight. I knew I couldn't waste valuable time. I had to find Simon. The medal had to wait.

Lamar and his friends escorted me safely to our camp, said goodbye, and quickly departed.

Chief sat on the ground next to his washtub, his face and arms uplifted to the sun.

Badger crawled out of his shebang. "I see Willy boy made it back from the Bake House alive. I thought the Raiders would have nabbed ya with your brother gone and all." He staggered forward with wobbly legs.

I stepped away from the soured whisky-breath. "Where's Simon?"

"I might trade ya something for news about your brother," Badger said. "Whatcha got to trade?"

My foot twitched. I wanted to kick Badger right in his bow-legged crotch. "Where's Simon?"

"Ain't ya heard?" He took a drink, wiped his mouth on his sleeve. "Locked in the Stocks with Tall Paul."

I bit my lip closed.

"The Tribe's dropping off like flies. You're surprising me, Willy boy," Badger said. "Tougher than I thought ya were. Figured you'd be dead before the others." He took a pull from his bottle. "Want a drink?"

I stared Badger in the eye. Badger shrugged. "A man's got to do what it takes to survive. There's no escaping, boy. When death comes, ya can't outrun it. No one survives. You're in Hell itself."

I looked around Badger at Chief. Chief still stared up at the sun in silence.

"Your eyes burn for the living, but there's no life to see. Ya came here to die, Willy boy. Face up to it. Ya ain't got what it takes. You're like the others, too soft." Badger extended his bottle. "Go ahead, have a drink, it'll ease the pain."

Badger's words made me feel prickly, like a snake trying to shed its skin.

"Suit yourself," Badger said. "I'm off to trade." He wobbled away.

I gulped a deep breath, and ran over to Chief.

"Where's Buckeye?" I said.

Chief's eyelids closed tight, his neck tilted toward the sinking sun; so strange not to see him scrubbing.

A body lay next to him, covered with Simon's blue woolen blanket.

"Chief," I said.

Chief's face was locked on the sun. "Chief, you're going to hurt your eyes." I squatted down next to the covered body. "Don't face the sun like that."

The big Indian tried to open flittering eyelids, but they were stuck shut. "See no more dead."

I scratched my head trying to think of something to say. I remembered how all the old-timers showered Simon with food when he lied to them about General Sherman being close by.

"Sherman!" I said. "Sherman's coming, Chief." I paused. "I read a newspaper in the Bake House. Rebs are scared. Sherman's coming, by golly. He'll be here soon."

Chief lowered his head. His brow was boiled with raw-pink blisters and his eyes were swollen slits.

"I'll be playing *Yankee Doodle Dandy* on my fife when Sherman comes through those gates." My fife was poking me in my ribs. I lifted my shirt up, and saw at least four Graybacks scurrying around. "Want to play a game of Even-odd with me?"

Chief shook his leathery face.

"I've got plenty of lice now." I pulled my fife out of my trousers and pointed it at the stockade gates. "Sherman's coming through those gates, Chief. You can count your lucky stars on that."

"Sherman." Chief touched around the top of his swollen eyes.

"Bet my fife on it." I turned my head to the body. I hated to look under the blanket, but had to. I peeled the blue wool back slowly. "Buckeye." I sighed and covered him back up.

"Not Buckeye." I felt raw inside. I wanted to feel something for Buckeye, but there was nothing left.

"Chief," I said. "Look at me." I sat down next to the big Indian. "Badger's a traitor. He's the one who told Wirz about the tunnel. I know it was Badger, heard him with my own ears, saw him with my eyes."

"Fix Badger for good this time," Chief said.

I didn't know what Chief meant, but I imagined it would not be good for Badger. "We got to get out of here, Chief. Somehow, I have to get Simon out."

"Sherman's coming?" Chief asked.

"That's right, Chief. Sherman is coming. He's breaking through Atlanta soon. May take a few days, though. Sherman's marching all the way to Savannah. The new men at the Bake House say Uncle Billy fights like an Indian. Union soldiers are sneaking all over the Georgia hillsides."

Chief continued to touch around his eyes.

"Simon and Tall Paul can't wait on Sherman though," I said. "They'll die in this heat. I've got to set them free!"

"We sleep tonight," Chief said.

"All right, Chief. We sleep."

CHAPTER ELEVEN

Outside the stockade, an eerie hoot sounded like it was deep in a thicket. My eyes were as wide as an owl's; I couldn't sleep a wink. I was bunking with Chief inside his shebang for safety. In the distance, drunken singing echoed like it escaped from the bottom of a well. *Was it Badger?*

Soon the singing muffled the sound of the owl. "Hooray, Hooray," Badger slurred. "In Dixieland, I'll take my stand, to live or die in Dixie..." Metal clanked. I heard a thump, a thud, and a laugh.

I eased to the front of the shebang on my belly. Badger sat crossed-leg on the ground next to the empty cooking kettle with his neck tilted up toward a moon as round as a cannon ball. "See that girl standing there, she's not as pregnant as she seems, she's just full of butter beans," Badger sang.

I heard Chief's heavy breathing and glanced behind me. Bright moonbeams shined through a crack in the top of the shebang and illuminated Chief's blistered face. He sat erect like a predator tracking the sound of its prey. His eyelids were too sunburned to open. His head moved in the direction of the sounds.

"It's Badger," I whispered.

Chief pushed me. His wide, brown face showed no emotion; he crept out of the shebang, turning his head slightly from left to right. I poked my head out. "By cracky, Chief," Badger said. "Ya ain't scrubbing at midnight are ya?" He took a long guzzle of whisky. "Been down brewing Pine-Top with the Boston boys all evening."

Chief stepped closer.

"Chief, your face looks awful. Can ya see okay?"

Chief reached out and swallowed Badger with his big bear arms.

"Chief, whatcha doing? Let go! You're breaking my blasted ribs…"

Badger's feet clanked the cooking kettle. I crawled all the way outside. Chief's shadow smothered Badger's squirming form. Badger's legs kicked like a dangling toad.

"Watch it! Ya can't see… gettin' awful close to the Deadline," Badger warned.

Like iron train wheels on straight tracks, Chief moved blindly forward.

"No, Chief! Wrong way. Got a cigar for ya in my shebang."

I bit my lip to keep from crying out. Chief couldn't see; he might stumble across the Deadline. He stopped just shy of it, and slung Badger like a big fish three feet beyond the rail.

Badger landed with a thud, popped up on his knees. Moonbeams shined on black barrels from the pigeon-roost.

"No! No boys!" Badger begged. "Got somethin' for ya. Buttons with hens!"

A shot rang out.

Badger flopped backward. He squirmed on the ground, but couldn't rise.

A sliver of moonlight slid off Chief's emotionless face. He shuffled his feet back to his shebang like an old man.

I crawled far back inside the shebang and closed my eyes tight. For the first time, I felt no pity for the dead; I hated Badger for being a traitor. I hated Badger worse than the Rebels.

That night, after tossing and turning for what seemed like hours, I finally fell asleep and dreamt I was standing on a dock. I watched a boat made from a split wooden canteen float on a coal-black lake. The boat was no bigger than a cupped leaf. Leroy and Lola were on board, happily frolicking around. A giant Hoosier playfully pushed the boat back and forth with a fingertip. I looked over Hoosier's shoulder. A sudden wave crashed the little craft away from the dock, out of Hoosier's reach. "Help! Help Leroy and Lola!"

I dove headfirst into the water. I pierced the blackness like an arrow. Down, down, down into the water I traveled. I suddenly stopped. For a split moment I panicked not knowing which way was up or down. I swam hard under the water, stroking far in front of my face until my arms broke the surface. I swallowed gulps of air. My feet kicked to keep afloat. I shook drops of water from my eyes and spotted the boat.

I swam hard. Each stroke splashed the boat further away from my grasp. I glanced over my shoulder. Whisking fog blurred my sight, but I could see that someone stood on the dock. *Was it Hoosier?*

"Help us!" I called.

The person leaped into a rowboat and rowed toward me. Leroy and Lola were gone. *Could it be Simon rowing?* Fog swirled across the surface. My chest and shoulders bobbed up and down like a sinking buoy. The angular jaw of the rower's face looked familiar, but it wasn't Simon or Hoosier.

The shadowy rower reached out an arm, but instead of pulling me aboard the boat, the stranger plunged into the water with me. My arms thrashed wildly. I grasped for anything solid to hold onto. The rower wrapped his arms and legs around me like a fishing net.

I sank further and further into the darkness. Fast-spewing air bubbles rushed from my lips. I knew we were so deep now I wouldn't have enough air in my lungs to make it back to the surface. In order to save the last of my air, I stopped struggling.

Deeper, deeper into the darkness I dropped. I hit the bottom like an anchor. Cold muck seeped around my ankles. I exploded in a burst of desperation, and ripped myself free. Strong fingers snagged my pant leg like barbed fishhooks, and pulled me back into the muck.

I looked up. Streaks of sunshine penetrated the depths of blackness. I got a glimpse of the face: *Father? It couldn't be! Why would he drown me?*

I kicked like a mule, squirmed, shoved off with all my power, and broke free. I pulled and pushed my way through the thick pressure. With the surface now within my grasp, I managed to take a gulping breath without water getting into my lungs. The air helped. Bubbles spewed. I stroked and kicked one final time, and my face broke the smothering surface. I shook the blindness from my eyes. Now I could see a watery image of Simon standing on the dock with his hands outreached. I tried to scream Simon's name, but only moldy lake water spat past my lips.

I woke up, wet with sweat. My mouth was dry.

"Bad spirits." Chief flipped over on his other side. I touched Chief's firm back with my fingertips. A dream. It was only a dream. My heart pounded out a rapid beat. I reached over, patted around and found the canteen, smelled it, and took a long gurgling gulp of warm water.

Next morning, I sat staring into the black coffee swishing around in my tin cup. I pressed my fingertip over a pinhole-size leak.

Chief sat beside me sorting a pile of laundry mostly by feel alone, his eyelids still blistered closed. I glanced over at Buckeye's stiff body still under the blanket. I wished I could feel sorrow for Buckeye, but didn't. I felt numb, like a shell had exploded nearby, shocking my senses into hiding.

I could only think about the nightmare. *What did it mean? Why was Father trying to drown me? What was the dream trying to tell me?* I glanced over at the Deadline; Badger's body was gone. *Did Chief do something with it?* I didn't bother to ask. I stood, and poured my coffee out. "I've got to get Simon out of the Stocks, Chief."

"Sherman come soon," Chief said.

"Can't wait for Sherman. Simon won't last another day in this heat."

"You go, I stay," Chief said. "I wait for Sherman. Take Simon's blanket, all you want of Badger's, too."

"You sure?" I glanced over at the blue woolen blanket covering Buckeye. I didn't want to see Buckeye's face. "You keep the blanket. You might need it until Sherman gets here."

"Take what you want." Chief pointed by memory to Badger's shebang.

"No thanks. I can't accept a thing that belonged to that traitor!"

Chief shook his head, fumbled with a ragged shirt in his washtub. "Badger dead, you want to live; take all you can get."

I nodded, stepped over, and hesitantly crawled inside Badger's shebang. The interior stank like Badger's Pine-Top whisky breath. My eyes widened when I spotted Badger's stash of treasures. Badger had blankets, clothes, haversacks, and food. First I picked a faded blue haversack. It was full of empty glass bottles. I rummaged through the food: turnips, potatoes, radishes, carrots. I kept searching.

"Simon's knife!" I picked up the Arkansas toothpick. Badger didn't miss a beat. Somehow he had managed to get the knife back. I kept digging around. Underneath an old shirt, I found Badger's looking glass. I crawled outside the entrance and peered through the glass at two old guards chatting on the pigeon-roost. *This too might come in handy.* I dumped the empty glass bottles out of the haversack and placed the looking glass inside of it. I also found four buttons with hens, three cigars, and a tin cup full of coffee beans hidden at the bottom of the haversack.

When I finally crawled back outside, I had more supplies in my new haversack than I'd had when I came into the camp. It felt good to be stocked up. I managed a wry smile when I spotted Chief scrubbing again, despite his blindness. "We're going to make it, Chief!" I ran my palm down the side of my fife. "You can come visit us in Kentucky. I'll play a lot of songs for you. Father will like you too, Chief."

I sighed deeply, hoping that I would find Father after saving Simon.

Chief said nothing. He scrubbed.

I tucked my fife deep inside the haversack. I slid the Arkansas toothpick up my sleeve to hide it. I cupped my hand and let the tip of the blade stick past the end of my knuckles.

In my other hand, I held up my canteen and took a big gulp. I thought of Simon. *How much longer would he last without water?*

Hooves clomped, and mules snorted. The Dead Wagon stopped in front of Chief. "Lamar!" I rushed forward. Lamar was driving the wagon. He slashed his finger under his throat signaling me to keep quiet. He pointed to the knoll in camp. I could tell that he wanted me to meet him there. I nodded, shrugged, but said nothing. I took a slow sip from the canteen and watched Lamar and another slave load Buckeye's body onto the wagon.

"Goodbye, Buckeye," I said. "Got lots of buttons with hens. You'd be proud of me." I thumped the top button on my coat, adjusted my sack on my back, and stepped out into Main. "Goodbye, Chief." I felt sad knowing I might never see Chief again. "Goodbye," I said again.

Chief continued his work as if he couldn't hear me.

I saluted Chief, and headed for the high ground to meet Lamar.

I stopped at the Stinks first to pee. The swamp-like ground around me was a soup of feces, flies, and maggots. I cupped my free hand over my nose and mouth, only taking in short breaths of the rancid air.

A man moaned from behind me. I quickly snapped up my trousers, wheeled around, and came face-to-face with Fog Eye!

Doubled-over, Fog Eye could barely stand. At first, I stumbled backward, nearly stepping into the Stinks. I recovered my balance and instantly slid the Arkansas toothpick out and gripped the handle, ready to fight. "Stay away from me! I'll use this knife if I have to!"

Fog Eye dropped to his knees. "Papa, help me home to Mama!"

I slid the knife back under my sleeve. Fog Eye's cheeks were purple and swollen. His bad eye rolled around in its socket like yoke in a cracked eggshell. Thick, yellow pus oozed from the badly injured eye.

I craned my head to get a better view, but I couldn't look too long at the grotesque eye. I could see part of Father's medal.

"Water, Papa," Fog Eye said. "Give me a drink, please Papa."

The medal was finally within my reach. It was matted in chest hair and dried blood around Fog Eye's neck. I stepped closer, bent down, and reached for it. I turned my head so that I didn't have to look at the wounded eye. I pushed forward, patting around the damp, corpse-like skin.

When my fingertips touched the leather bootlace that held the medal, I jerked it off Fog Eye's neck with one swift pull.

"It's me, Joseph." Fog Eye reached for my hand. "Hold my hand, Papa."

I eased three steps away from Fog Eye and sat down on the ground. I slowly ran my fingers over the familiar smoothness of the medal. "Father, where are you?" I said. I glanced back at Fog Eye and sighed in sorrow. My pity for Fog Eye instantly faded, and a flash of anger raced through my veins. I stood, stomped over, and shoved him over on his back. I straddled his chest with wide spread legs. "Where'd you get this?"

Fog Eye rolled his neck back and forth moaning.

"Where did you get this medal?" I shouted.

"Water. You promised me water."

"I didn't promise you anything." I summoned the courage to look directly into what was left of the man's eyes. The good eye was as blank and void as the fogged eye. It was like looking into the lifeless eyes of a corpse.

I shook my head, opened the lid of my canteen, and tilted the water so Fog Eye could drink. He gulped the water, spilling it down his chin.

"That's enough." I pulled the canteen from his thirsty lips, and set the water just out of his reach.

"Where did you get this medal?" I asked.

"Grave digging detail," Fog Eye said. "I didn't steal it,

Papa, I promise."

I grabbed his neck with both hands. "I don't believe you." I squeezed hard. The flesh sunk between my fingers. Fog Eye's face flashed red, and faded to purple. Fresh pus oozed from his eye. His throat still moved as if he were gurgling water.

"What good does it do?" a weak voice said from behind me.

I twisted around. It was the little man I had first encountered in the camp eating worms. He still had his digging spoon. "The dead-dead are better off than the living-dead," the man said. He popped a fresh worm into his mouth. "You'll do him a favor to kill him."

I pressed Fog Eye's head hard against the earth. "Please," Fog Eye pleaded. His fingers wiggled for water. "Water, please."

Out of mercy, I grabbed the canteen, and gave him another drink. I grasped hold of the knife handle, pulled it out, and plunged the blade hard into the dirt next to Fog Eye's chest. "Was the man you took the medal from alive or dead?"

"Dead," Fog Eye said. "More water, please."

I sighed, and shook the canteen. There was only enough for one last drink. I handed him the canteen, and asked, "What did the man look like?"

"Dead men in a pile all look alike."

"Was he an officer?"

Fog Eye tried to rise, but didn't have the strength.

"Did he have an officer's uniform?" I said. "Did he have red hair?"

Fog Eye shook his head and shrugged.

My questions were wasting time. I had to find Lamar. I had to help Simon.

Fog Eye lay with his eyes closed. His chest heaved in and out. I had heard this kind of breathing many times over the past few years. Death would come soon. I reached inside the haversack, found a potato and carrot, and gave them to the worm-eating man.

"Want a worm?" The man held up a yellow grub.

"No thanks." I said.

I made my way through tightly spaced shebangs to the high-ground where I was to meet Lamar. It was the same small knoll where I had first scouted the camp for signs of my fife with Simon.

Lamar wasn't here yet. I pulled the looking glass out, and scanned the camp. Off in the distance, I spotted the Stocks. Two slaves were straining to load Tall Paul onto the Dead Wagon. Tall Paul's enormous frame looked like a fallen tree. "No! Tall Paul. Simon!" Simon's head was moving, trying to turn his neck to look at Tall Paul. Simon's face was streaked in dirt and sweat. His eyes looked propped open by thin sticks of fear.

"Simon!" I crammed the looking glass back into the sack, and scrambled down the hill to the Stocks. "Simon!"

When I reached my brother, Simon managed to cock his head in the direction of my voice. Simon opened his eyes. His bent arms wiggled like broken wings. He tried to speak, but only a dry cough came out.

"We'll make it, Simon." I pressed Father's medal on his cheek. "I've got Father's medal! I'm going to find him! You'll make it, Simon. You'll make it!"

A guard shoved me. "Shut that up! Get away from here or I'll lock you up!"

I twisted around with clenched fists. "That's my brother!"

The guard jabbed his bayonet into the ground between my legs. "I don't care if it's the son of God. You want to get cruci-fied with him?"

My fist stayed clenched; I couldn't take my eyes off Simon.

"Let him go!" I lunged at the guard.

The guard lunged back with his bayonet.

A strong grip snagged the back of my haversack and pulled me away. It was Quick Jim. "Come with me, Will, Lamar's hunting for you."

CHAPTER TWELVE

Quick Jim and I waited for Lamar at the top of the knoll. I sat crossed-legged with Father's medal in my hand and traced my fingertip across the smooth spot. Every few minutes, I picked up the looking glass, and checked on Simon. Simon's eyes were closed. "No movement, not even a twitch," I said, glancing over to Quick Jim. "It's hard to tell if he's alive or dead."

"He's alive," Quick Jim said. "Don't worry. Simon won't be visiting the Dead House today."

I lowered my looking glass. "When we get back to Kentucky, the first thing I'm going to do with Simon is swim in Wilson's Spring."

"I reckon it's a nice cool dip," Quick Jim said.

"It's cool all right." I wiped sweat from my brow with the back of my hand. "Father sits under the willow shade tree, whittling fishing sticks for us." I raised the looking glass to my eye and watched Simon. *I hoped his stillness was just sleep.*

"The deep spring water's bone cold," I said. "The bank's covered with green watercress and black moss covers the rocks. I like to watch the water bugs skedaddle across the surface..."

"Dead House," a voice said.

Startled, I jumped up, dropped the looking glass, twisted around, and came face-to-face with Lamar. "You're like a cat, Lamar. Always sneaking up on people."

"The Dead House is the way out for Simon," Lamar said. "Teamsters drivin' wagon talks of a ghost that ups and runs away like a Yankee Jesus they says."

"Ghost?" I questioned.

Quick Jim stood too.

Lamar chuckled. "Ain't no such thing as a ghost. A man plays possum. He fakes dead to get loaded on the Dead Wagon. He gets taken to the Dead House outside the wall. Once it's dark, he rises up and runs for the woods."

"Ghost. I get it," Quick Jim said. "Yankee ghost, I like it. We got Yankee moles, too. There's moles digging out of here as we speak." Quick Jim picked up the looking glass and scanned the woods outside the stockade. "My men are going under the wall tonight."

"Tonight!" I said. "I thought Captain Wirz found your tunnel."

"He found a tunnel, not that tunnel. We had three going. One under the Bake House was a decoy, didn't go anywhere. The tunnel Wirz found Simon digging in is called 'Old Glory'. The tunnel we're going out of is 'Uncle Billy'. Quick Jim pointed over the stockade wall with the looking glass.

"Uncle Billy will open up like a shallow grave about fifty paces from those pines."

I looked over to the guards on the pigeon-roost. "The guards can see that far."

"We're going to distract them with a baseball game tonight." Quick Jim smiled. "We're lighting torches, and playing a night game. We got the guards all worked up and excited about placing bets on the two teams. The Rebs love it! While they're hooting and hollering about the game, my men will be popping out of their exit holes like moles and running for the woods."

I smiled at the thought of little moles digging.

"My friends, Spotswood and Jocko, drive the Dead Wagon," said Lamar, and put his hand on my shoulder. "Come dusk, your brother will play dead, and I'll hide him away on the Dead Wagon."

"Why?" I asked. "Why take the risk for us?"

"My boy was whipped to death at your age," Lamar said. His deep brown eyes clouded. "I can see him in you."

I sighed, and lifted Father's medal from my neck. "Take this." I slowly extended the medal to Lamar's hand. "I trust you. Show it to Simon. Tell him I'm waiting for him at the Dead House. He'll trust you too, when he sees this."

Lamar nodded, wrapped the leather string around the medal, and stuck it in his pocket. "I'll lay him thick in the dead. Look for a lantern on a shovel shaft. That's where Simon will be. When the lights go out, crawl to it! I'll meet you there."

"Shovel shaft," I said. "When the light goes out, go to it."

"Go to the Dead House right away," Quick Jim said. "Ask the guard to let you speak with Atwater. Tell him I sent you to volunteer to bury the dead."

"Who is he?" I said.

"He's Clerk of the Dead. He was paroled to manage the Dead List. Got a detailed list of almost every man that's died here. At dusk, when everyone leaves the Dead House, you hide in a safe place."

"Understand the plan?" Lamar asked.

"Atwater at the Dead House," I answered. "He keeps the Dead List. Hide. Look for the lantern and shovel shaft."

"Good boy." Quick Jim patted my shoulder. "We'll all meet up in the thick of the woods. Follow this hoot owl call." Jim cupped his hands. "Whoo-whoo. Whoo-whoo."

I nodded. I had heard this call before.

"There's a lot of work to finish," Quick Jim said. "Will, be sure you stick to the plan. Don't get in any trouble today. Go right to the Dead House and ask for Atwater."

"I will," I said.

Quick Jim squeezed my shoulder and smiled. He scrambled down the knoll, and disappeared into a crowd of men.

Lamar lowered his head and winked at me.

"Thank you, Lamar." I reached out and touched the back of Lamar's rough hand.

"Don't you worry none," Lamar said. "There's a lot of good folks going to see you and your brother home."

Down the hill, and into the center of Main, I walked with my head lowered. I did worry though. I worried about Father.

"Hey, boy," a man called. "What ya got to trade in that haversack?"

I didn't look back. I quickened my pace. "Dead List," I said to myself and marched on in a daydream-like trance. Hundreds of dead Union-soldier faces muffled my thoughts. Voices of men lulled in my skull. I saw Father's face among the dead. Every other face, Father's face. I tried to wipe it from my mind by shaking my head, but couldn't.

I sat down on the edge of Main, leaned back on my haversack, and looked up at the sun directly above me. "Midday," I said. "A lot of looking time until dusk." *Where would Father be? What did the drowning dream mean?*

Thick, fast-moving clouds rushed in from the West like battle formations. Two clouds collided into one. *Two becoming one. Simon and Father as one*, I thought. "That's it! Father was trying to save me," I said. "He can't swim. He can't swim a lick. That's why he always whittled under the willow at the spring. He can't swim! Father jumped into the water to save me. He drowned to save me!"

A shot rang out from the direction of the Tribe's camp. "Chief?" I sat erect, wiped at my eyes. "I hope that wasn't Chief." I stood, took several quick steps toward the Tribe, but stopped. "If I don't make it to the Dead House, Simon will surely die. I have to follow the plan. I have to get to the Dead House!"

When I got to the South Gates, I found a lone sentry guarding the road to the Dead House. I approached the old, slouchy guard one small step at a time. Not six feet from him, I took a deep breath, and said, "I need to get to the Dead House; I'm late for the grave digging crew."

"No live men through the gate today, Captain's orders." The old guard straightened his slouch.

"I have to get through to see Mr. Atwater!"

"You ain't dead, and you ain't going to the Dead House unless I shoot ya!"

Head lowered, I stared at the ground.

"Get on out of here!" the guard shouted. "I can't let ya stand near the gate."

I walked a few yards away and sat down with my chin tucked to my chest. I had to get to Atwater somehow. Off in the distance, a buzzard squawked. "Buttons with hens!" I poked a stiff finger down my chest. "One, two, three, four hens on my coat, and four in my pocket."

I stood and strutted back to the guard with an open palm

full of buttons. "I've got four buttons with hens!"

The guard eyed the hens with raised brows. "Four buttons ain't no count to open the gate and get me shot."

"They're real nice hens," I said. "Here take one. See for yourself."

The guard held the button to his chest as if he were trying it on.

"It's nice, isn't it?" I said.

The guard smiled. "Reckon it is."

"The guard at the North gates wants to trade me a barber's kit for all eight of them." I snatched back the button the guard held, and stuck it in my pocket. "He's a real nice feller, even offered to teach me how cut hair." I ran my fingers through my scruffy hair. "Barbers do real well inside the prison."

"Ya say ya got eight hens?" The guard's grin widened.

"Oh yeah," I said. "Four in my pocket." I patted my leg. "And four on my jacket." I thumped my thumb down my chest touching all four buttons.

"All right," the guard said. "I'll take 'em." He looked around. "Come quick. Take off your jacket and I'll cut them off fast."

Once inside, I pulled my jacket closed over my chest and crossed my arms tight. The Dead House sat far back near the woods. Row upon row of dead men lined head-to-head and toe-to-toe formed a path to the house. A putrid stench like a decaying buffalo carcass hung over the top of the dead. I paused when I thought I saw eyes moving on some of the corpses. *Were they faking dead?* I looked closer, and saw that it was only scurrying flies, and ants scavenging. *What if Father is here? What if he's buried here?*

I gagged, and lowered my head. My mouth filled with warm spit. I coughed and heaved, but nothing came up. I forced myself forward. "Even though I walk through the shadow of death, I fear no evil; for thou art with me; Thy rod and Thy staff comfort me…"

Out of the corner of my eye, I spied red hair, and stopped. An open-earth trench grave about four feet deep was filled with bodies laid side-by-side. I peered more closely and sighed in relief. "Thank goodness, that's not him." A thin layer of dirt smothered the open mouth of a man with red hair.

"Some say a man dies every eleven minutes," a voice said. "Don't have pine boxes for none of 'em."

I spun around and cringed at the sight of a toothless boy. He looked like he had been dipped in dirt, and only his eyes and mouth had been dusted off.

"One day, one hundred and thirty men died." The boy swung his shovel gesturing to the fields. "Almost ten thousand dead men out here already."

"Where did you get that shovel?" I asked. I imagined Simon lying thick in the dead with the boy's shovel marking his spot.

A loud crack made me jump. I turned around to see a young rebel guard bashing a dead man's mouth with his rifle butt. The guard reached between the lips and pulled out a bloody gold tooth. He wiped it clean on his shirt, stuck it in his pocket, and moved on to the next mouth.

"Poor Rebels are the worst kind of battlefield rag-pickers," the boy said.

I rubbed my lower jaw, glad I didn't have any gold in my mouth. "Where's Atwater?"

The boy leaned on his shovel and pointed far down the row of the dead.

"Thank you." I walked to the man, and stood watching him read small tags that were attached to many of the corpses' toes.

"Excuse me," I said.

Atwater didn't look up. He scribbled on worn yellow paper.

"Excuse me, Mr. Atwater."

Atwater raised his head partway. His body looked young, but lines and wrinkles etched and crossed his face in scars of sleepless worries. "What is it? What do you want?"

All I could think about was Father. *Was he here?*

"Want a job?" Atwater shoved a piece of paper and a pencil into my hands. "Look for the bodies with toe-tags. Write down the name, the regiment, and the cause of death on the paper."

I stared at the paper, lifted my chin. "Quick Jim sent me."

Atwater looked right through me with sullen eyes that had seen thousands of dead men. "What do you want?"

"I want, I want…"

"Go ahead, boy," Atwater said. "Spit it out."

I swallowed hard. "I want a name. I want to search for a name."

"Maybe your name is out there among the unmarked graves." Atwater fanned his arm pointing to a sea of dead men. "Grab yourself a shovel! Good luck digging for a name. There's over four hundred unmarked graves! Let me know when you find it, I'll put it on my list."

"My Father!" My voice trembled. "It's my Father's name. Taylor, from Kentucky, an officer."

Atwater's gaze softened. His blue eyes sat far back in his skull. I could now see a younger man as Atwater's jaw loosened and his shoulders slightly drooped.

"You can see my Master List. Got to warn you though. You won't find what you're looking for; nobody does."

Atwater pulled from his inside coat pocket a wide cylinder of tightly bound yellowed papers and extended it to me.

"Thank you," I said, gently taking the roll.

"I'll need it back soon," Atwater said. "There's a lot of names to add today. Heat's taking men like the Devil."

"I'll hurry," I said.

CHAPTER THIRTEEN

Sun-washed streaks of reds and blues cast long shadows across the Dead House grounds. I shielded my eyes and tried to read the time of day by the length of the shadows. "Well past noon," I said, and shifted the Dead List between my hands. "It's heavy as a loaf of hot-baked bread. I've got to hurry!"

I walked behind the Dead House and found a clear spot to sit down between picks and shovels. I looked at my feet; no shadow. I would read until the sun passed over the Dead House. Careful not to tear the pages, I gently unrolled them. The soiled paper was dirty, and blotted with what looked like dots of dried sweat. With a deep breath I blew a fine layer of gritty dust off of the first page. The dust smelled like the ink of an old newspaper.

With a quick glance, I examined the first page. The names appeared to be listed by grave numbers. I sighed. "Thousands, thousands of names and numbers and they're not listed in alphabetical order. If Taylor is on here, I might never find it."

I skipped around the numbers and names quickly reading as many as I could on the first few pages. I randomly flipped through several pages hoping that I would not find the name Taylor. The more I looked, the better I felt. I didn't want to find Father on this list. Lost in the shadows of time, I read numbers and names, numbers and names...

"Are you done? Atwater said. "I need that list back."

I jumped, and looked up. Atwater wiped dirty sweat from his brow with his sleeve. "You've been looking for over two hours," he said.

A long shadow stretched from Atwater's feet. "Please give me more time!" I pleaded. "I need more time!"

Atwater shook his head, and walked away.

I skipped forward several pages and read out loud: "One thousand and twenty one, Oates; one thousand and eighty-five, Marshall; two thousand and three, Emerson..."

I stopped, glanced over to the nearby dead men piled at the side of the Dead House. They looked like stacked logs ready for a long winter. Their blank faces were ready to be buried inside the earth forever. *Who are these men? Why are so many dead? What for? Freeing slaves? Saving the Union?*

I sighed, closed my eyes, opened them again; I ran my index finger down the names fast, searching for any "Ts" in Taylor, page after page, page after page. My eyes were damp with panic. Not even a thread of a clue was yielded, only blurry numbers and letters. I closed my eyes, my mind clouded, my breaths quickened. "Nine thousand, six hundred names!"

Faster, faster I scanned the numbers and names lost in shifting sands of time. When I looked up, the sun had crested past the Dead House grounds and touched the top of tall pines in the woods. I closed my eyes and lightly bounced the back of my head against the Dead House wall. The impact brought freedom from the stiffness of searching. "Three years," I said.

"It's been three years since Father left Kentucky."

I thought of the early autumn day that I first put on my army uniform. The air outside was as crisp and blue as the Union colors. My new jacket fit as tight as an ironed tablecloth. My gold eagle buttons were like coins from a treasure. I strutted around the house that day with my fife tilted high, practicing battle calls. Later that same day, I walked nearly seven miles to Becky Adam's farm. For over an hour, I marched back and forth past her huge property. I know she saw me. I saw her peeking out the curtains of her bedroom window. Oh, how I wanted her to come outside and see me up close. I waived to her. She didn't waive back. She turned her back on me. That was the last time I saw Becky. If only Father could have seen my uniform when it was new.

"The day is done," Atwater said.

I snapped my eyes open and stood on wobbly legs, clutching the Dead List tightly to my chest. "It's impossible to find one name among ten thousand!"

"Told you so," Atwater said. "I wish I could give you more time, but the day's done, can't get a minute back."

"There's too many cotton pickin' dead names!" I tossed the list to the ground. The pages sprawled apart.

"Hey, boy," Atwater said. "Be careful with those pages!"

Warm spit filled my mouth. I stumbled over to a trench lined with ready-to-be-covered bodies. With my head spinning, I heaved. Only drool rolled down my chin. I slowly rose, dizzily planting each step, trying to find my legs. "I've lost my Father. I've got to save my brother!"

Atwater shook his head and tightly rolled his papers back up. "If he's alive, you'll find each other; if he's dead, may you meet in Heaven."

I nodded, sat down, and pulled my fife out of my haversack. *Maybe he is alive?* My fingers trembled as my mouth blew out the sweet, sweet sound of *Amazing Grace.*

Nearby slaves stopped digging. The boy with the shovel came over and sat down next to me. The slaves joined in: "Amazing Grace, how sweet it is…"

Finally, I lowered my fife and looked around. I had no idea how long I had been playing. The slaves, Atwater, and the digging-boy all stared at me with wide eyes of admiration as if I had brought something to the graves from Heaven.

The final sliver of the day's sun slipped from the sky and vanished. Cool air carried a honeysuckle scent across the Dead House grounds. "I've never smelled anything so sweet before," I said to Atwater.

"The dead will do that for you." Atwater stretched his arms over his head. "The dead will make life come alive for you. You'll see, smell, taste, and touch like never before."

I smiled at the chirp of crickets chattering in the woods. "Time to go," Atwater said.

"I'm staying here," I said.

"You can't stay here all night, boy?"

"Quick Jim's orders," I said.

Atwater shook his head. "Stay in this area, no one comes back here after I leave." He smirked. "These are a happy bunch of dead fellows. Don't worry, you'll be safe here." He patted me on the shoulder and walked away.

"Thank you," I said, and silently crept over to a line of bodies. I found a gap between two men on the ground. I slid my haversack off, lay down flat on my back, and made myself stiff as a corpse.

Peace at last. It felt good to be dead. "Death isn't so bad after all," I whispered. *Death is nothing like I imagined.* I patted the kneecap of the man next to me. Death was so close-up now; I couldn't be scared. I tapped my foot to distant banjo music drifting over the stockade wall as I pictured Simon draped over bodies in the Dead Wagon. I hoped Simon was still alive.

"Father's not dead," I whispered to myself. "He's not on that list. He could be hiding in the woods. He might even be marching with Sherman at this very moment..." My rambling, disconnected thoughts seemed to follow the moonrise across the sky.

Stars filled the night with sparkles of hope. I tried to imagine that each bright star was a state. Here I was lying on my back in Georgia. All I had to do was hop to the Tennessee star, and then I was only one star away from Kentucky.

At home, I would have many chores to catch up on: planting, feeding, and chopping. I would still hate chopping, but I wouldn't complain to Father. Simon and I would hunt: squirrels, rabbits, and deer.

Aunt Kelly would make us her sweet potato pudding. The thought of it made my mouth water. I would have Aunt Kelly bake a batch of sweet potato pudding the size of a twelve-pound cannonball. We'd visit Cousin James for a picnic on the banks of the Ohio River.

A cheer suddenly erupted behind the stockade wall. I popped up on my knees. The glow of burning torches highlighted the shadowy figures of guards on the parapet jumping up and down with raised arms. "Hooray! Hooray!"

"The baseball game!" I said in a hush. I lay back down and listened to the cheers. I pictured Quick Jim's angular frame rounding the bases. The night passed on. My eyes grew heavy as bags of cornmeal.

A mule snorted. Startled, I sat up. Hooves clomped. I flattened back out, dead-quiet. The squeaky sound of turning wagon wheels came my way. I wanted to rise up, but was afraid it might be a guard on patrol. My breathing raced at a double-quick pace. Then, the soft voices of slaves singing reassured me. It had to be Lamar and his friends. I hoped Simon was okay.

Shadowy lantern light glowed close by. I heard a plop-ping of bodies hitting the ground like heavy sacks. The fast murmur of whispering voices sounded as if they wished to get away from the dead quickly. I slowly raised my head to see where the wagon was parked. Three dark figures tossed bodies off of the wagon.

I crouched back down in my hiding spot and listened to cheers from the baseball game.

"Whoo-whoo!" I heard the secret call and popped my head up like a gobbler. I couldn't see a living soul, but I saw the lantern light. The wagon and the three men were gone. The light flickered for only a moment, and vanished like someone had blown out the flame. "That's the sign," I said.

I had to keep low so the guards would not spot me. I crawled on my hands and knees over the tops of corpses. Some bodies were hard as stone. Some were soft like muck at the bottom of a bog. "Fear no evil, fear no evil," I chanted. I moved my hands as fast as I could over damp fluids and sticky substances.

I heard a moan and froze. I checked the pulse of the body beside me. It was cold as a steel saber. I heard the moan again! *Simon?*

I crouched low and squinted in the dark. Finally I spotted the faint, thin shaft of the shovel. I stood and crept toward it, stepping across bodies.

"Simon. Simon," I whispered. I spotted a bundle that looked like a body rolled up inside of a blanket. I reached out and touched scruffy wool. "Simon," I whispered. "You're alive."

Only Simon's head poked out from the blanket roll. His eyes were closed. His breathing sounded deep and heavy. I scrubbed Simon's hair with my fingernails and wished I had some water left to give my brother. I should have never wasted it on Fog Eye.

Out of the darkness, strong fingertips clasped the back of my neck. I jumped like the Devil had caught me trying to sneak out the back door of Hell.

"Lamar!"

Lamar placed his hand over my lips. "Hush up, boy." He pulled me low to the ground. "Simon's too weak to walk. We'll have to tote him to the woods."

I rapidly nodded.

"Spotswood, Jocko, come now," Lamar said.

I could see shadows of two men scurrying fast toward him.

Lamar hoisted Simon up and laid him across his wide shoulders. Father's medal dropped out from the bundle and dangled from Simon's neck. I reached for it, but it bounced away as Lamar toted and bumped like a pack mule.

A full moon rose in the starry Georgia sky. The tiny red embers of a guard's smoking pipe could be seen high on the parapet. Like goblins fresh from the graves, they scrambled through the Dead House grounds, and into the first clump of pine trees in the forest.

Loud dogs barked in the distance. Lamar dropped to his knees and lay Simon on the ground. Spotswood, Jocko, and Lamar spoke in hushed-quick words. I crawled on my belly to Simon and put my hand near his mouth to make sure he was still breathing. Only faint, baby breaths. The train whistle from Anderson Station howled in the distance. "Close," I whispered to Simon. "Hear that train? We're close."

A shot rang out. The loud barking dogs were much closer.

"Lordy!" Lamar raised up on his knees. "The tracking dogs are closing in on us." He dropped back down. "Men coming our way!" he whispered. "Don't move."

I held my breath. Simon moaned and I covered his mouth with a cupped hand to muffle the noise. Running footsteps thumped close by.

"Prisoners," Lamar said. "Quick Jim's moles are out!"

I rose up on my knees and saw the shadowy figures of at least five men scatter through the darkness.

"Those dogs are bred and reared for trackin' slaves," Lamar said. "Jocko and Spotswood will lead them off to the train depot. Hounds will follow their scent over ours. I'll see you to your hiding place."

"You can't, Lamar!" I tugged hard on his sleeve. "They'll lynch you if you get caught helping us."

"You listen to me, boy." Lamar pushed me back down. "Ain't no lynching me, I'm Mr. Wilcox property. They gotta get permission to lynch me. Mrs. Wilcox's is helping us. She's part of the Underground Railroad. You can't make it without me carrying your brother!"

A horse neighed. Tall flames sparked from the torches of galloping riders. I dropped to the ground and covered Simon with my body.

Spotswood and Jocko ran toward the train station. Their fleeing silhouettes vanished like lifting mist off a river. I stayed breathlessly still while barking dogs and horses passed only yards away.

The lonely train whistle howled. Three shots rang out from the direction of the tracks. The dogs stopped barking. "One more dead," I whispered. "What name goes on the list tonight? I hope it's not Spotswood or Jocko."

"Will," Simon moaned. "Will…"

"Simon!" I helped Simon raise his head up by placing both hands behind my brother's neck. "Simon, we're out! You're going to make it," I said looking Simon square in the eyes. "Don't give up. You're going to survive!"

CHAPTER FOURTEEN

When I opened my eyes I was inside a cabin as dark as a tomb. The smell of fresh manure hung thick in the air outside the cabin walls. I knew we were hiding on a farm. I remembered entering the cabin in the silence of night. I felt like I had been sleeping through a long dream. I reached over and felt Simon's arm. His breaths were raspy, but steady. I closed my eyes again.

I woke up next to the sound of a barnyard rooster crowing. Dawn streams of sunlight flitted through cracked wallboards on the eastern side of the cabin. The rooster crowed on and on for his troops to rise at daybreak. I heard hog grunts and snorts. Birds whistled secret notes. I tried to guess the type of birds they were by the different tones of their songs: mockingbird, sparrow, blue jay, chickadee, robin, I knew them all.

I heard humming and singing and smelled the unmistakable aroma of freshly cooked food. My mouth eagerly watered.

The cabin door creaked open. I had to shield my eyes from

the bright sunlight. When my eyes adjusted I was surprised to see a woman. She closed the door and lit a candle.

She was swaddled in layers and layers of white cotton robes. I looked more closely at her wrinkled face in the candlelight. Reflective pupils sat deep in ancient lines and wrinkles. She looked like she could have been a hundred years old.

She said few English words. Mostly she mumbled to herself in a strange language as she nursed Simon. She carried a crimson-colored handbag, and she endlessly pulled all kinds of herbs, roots, and potions from it. All of these things left strange smells in the cabin.

Before she left, she handed me a huge basket. "Thank you," I said. She bobbed her head. I knew we understood each other. I quickly rummaged through the basket. It had roast pork, salty ham, turkey, buttermilk biscuits, hardboiled eggs, potatoes, apples, peaches, and best of all fresh spring water. I tasted the water first. It was the sweetest water I had ever drunk. I imagined it came from a deep, deep well nearby. I lay down next to Simon. Steady breaths of hope escaped his lips.

The call of an owl woke me up during the night. I figured I had slept all day after eating too much food. Moonbeams shone through the cracks and reflected off of Father's medal around Simon's neck. *Where was Lamar?* I faintly remembered Lamar ushering Simon and me into this cabin.

The old woman swaddled in white came each morning with food. I counted the days by her visits. On the forth day, I had one eye pressed to a keyhole-size crack in a wallboard trying to see a bird when I heard, "Will! Where are we?"

Simon's clear words pricked my ears like a stiff, metal comb. I leapt over to my brother's side. "We're out!" I lifted Father's medal off Simon's chest. "We're out. Lamar helped us. We're in some cabin."

"Is Father dead?" Simon sat up.

I shook my head. "I don't know."

I heard women's voices off in the distance. Simon and I were silent, as the voices grew louder. I twisted my neck from side to side trying to better hear.

The cabin door creaked open. A flash of bright sunbeams blinded me. When my eyes adjusted I could see the silhouettes of a tall woman and a girl with floppy bonnets and cotton-white dresses.

"You still don't smell much better than the hogs," the woman said. She pulled the door slightly closed.

The partially blocked sunlight allowed my eyes to clearly see. Mrs. Wilcox stood erect as a Sunday school teacher. She carried a bundle under her arms. "Jonas and Dickwood are bringing hot water for baths and here are some clothes for you."

Mrs. Wilcox eased over and closed the door. "Lamar will be here soon. You'll be loaded into our market wagon and hidden between bales of cotton. The wagon will take you to the train station. The train takes our cotton to Savannah. Lamar will see you safely into the hands of the Underground Railroad in Savannah. They'll take you on a trading ship up the coast to Maryland. The end of your journey is close."

"What happened to Quick Jim?" I asked. "Did he get away?"

"He did," Mrs. Wilcox said.

I sighed in relief.

"I knew they couldn't catch Quick Jim," Simon said.

"Quick Jim should be half way to Boston by now," Mrs. Wilcox said. "Jim helped eight other men escape."

In my mind, I could see Quick Jim kicked-back on a bale of cotton deep in the belly of a schooner.

The girl removed her bonnet. I squinted hard to see her. Her auburn hair had a twilight glow in the flittering light. "The clothes should fit you. They belonged to my brothers." She smiled and bowed slightly. "I'm Susanna."

I felt an unusual stir tingle all over my body. I rubbed my sleeves like I had a bad itch. "I'm Will, Will Taylor."

She laughed. "I know who you are."

"I'm Simon!" Simon sat more erect.

"You look better, Simon," Mrs. Wilcox said. "Glady's medicine never fails. She's the best midwife in Georgia."

I couldn't take my eyes off of Susanna's hair.

"Who's in the bath first?" Mrs. Wilcox asked.

I didn't want to leave Susanna. "You go first," I said to Simon.

"You're dirtier than I am."

"Mother, may I show Will around the farm?" Susanna quickly asked.

Mrs. Wilcox raised her strong chin as she pondered the question. She looked at me.

I nervously shifted my feet.

"Don't stay gone too long," Ms. Wilcox said. "The market wagon will be ready soon."

Susanna grabbed my hand and pulled me outside the cabin. I felt as though I walked through a dream as Susanna spoke fast about her family farm and how she and her mother could go to prison for helping Union men escape. Her eye's sparkled with pride as she spoke.

I listened without a word spoken. I only wanted to hear her soft voice, not mine. I found myself already wishing for more time with her.

Suddenly, Susanna stopped talking. She looked me in the eye. "I have something for you." She reached inside her pocket and pulled out an envelope. "I want you to remember me."

I lowered my head and slowly opened the envelope. It held several locks of auburn hair. When I raised my head, Susana leaned forward and kissed me square on my lips.

The inside of my body instantly rushed with warmth.

"You're very brave, Will Taylor. I hope we meet again."

"I won't forget you," I said. "I'll play a song on my fife every day just for you."

Off in the distance, the train whistle from Anderson Station howled three sharp cries. I cocked my head and looked closely at Susanna. She smiled. I saw peace in her eyes. I took a deep breath, and strength filled my chest. I wished that she could see me in a clean uniform with shiny new buttons. She wouldn't turn her back on me like Becky Adams did.

I knew that Simon and I would make it home to Kentucky. I also knew that I might never see Father again. I felt very sad about this, but I was not alone. So much had been lost by so many on both sides of the war.

"While inside the prison," I said. "I believed that all Rebels were evil for letting us starve to death. But the Raiders proved there are bad men in the Union too."

I stepped closer to Susanna and touched her hair. She leaned on me. "You and your mother proved that there are good people everywhere. Someday, I'll come back to Georgia and find you," I said. "We'll all be free. All people, black and white will travel the country without fear."

AUTHOR'S NOTE

Boys as young as nine years old participated in the Civil War. We have no accurate records of how many boys enlisted for the Northern or Southern armies. Over four hundred thousand were involved directly in the conflict. National laws now prevent boys from participating in American wars.

Andersonville was one of the largest Confederate military compounds. More than forty-five thousand Union soldiers were confined here. Over thirteen thousand men died within the prison walls from disease, malnutrition, and gross over-crowding conditions.

Thanks to a young man named Dorence Atwater who kept a detailed "List of the Dead," there were only four hundred and sixty unmarked graves. Clara Barton, founder of the American Red Cross, was also instrumental in helping Dorence Atwater protect the Andersonville cemetery at the end of the Civil War.

Andersonville Prison is now a National Historic Site; and

the National Park System has honored it by designating its hallowed grounds to serve as a memorial to all American prisoners of war. The site has an award-winning lesson plan for teaching about historical places.

Visit boysread.org to be the first to get a copy of *The Bird*.
The Bird is a mysterious and enchanting novel that boys will love.

Our mission is to transform boys into lifelong
readers. We are an organization of parents, educators,
librarians, mentors, authors, and booksellers.

http://www.boysread.org/